David Park is a teacher in a country school in County Down. He is thirty-eight years old, was born in Belfast, and lived there till seven years ago.

THE HEALING

DAVID PARK

PHŒNIX

A Phoenix paperback
First published in Great Britain by Jonathan Cape in 1992
This paperback edition published in 1993 by Phoenix,
a division of Orion Books Ltd,
Orion House, 5 Upper St Martin's Lane,
London WC2H 9EA

A CIP catalogue record for this book is available
from the British Library

ISBN 1 85799 095 1

Printed and bound in Great Britain by
The Guernsey Press Co. Ltd, Guernsey, C.I.

For the children afflicted by dreams

SILENTLY, AND FACE down, he scuttled like a rat along the damp course of the ditch, trying to find its deepest safest spot. His toes and sharp-pointed knees gouged soft furrows in the matted bed of leaf mould. Tiny drops of water sprayed on to his back as he burrowed through the tangled wetness of beaded grass. He paused for a second and angled his seed-sprinkled head to listen. It was still coming. Curling tightly into a knot he closed his eyes. It was coming closer all the time. An insect flitted across his hand and dampness seeped into his skin but he held himself still and silent as a stone while the steady tick tick tick unwound towards him. It was almost level now and he could hear the squeak of the saddle and the whirr of the wheels as it laboured along the lane. The sounds tightened slowly round him like a noose, blocking out even the incessant beating of his heart. He waited motionless until they had faded then carefully raised his head to the top of the ditch and peered through a curtain of tousled grass as the black-coated figure hunched over

I

the handlebars struggled up the rise and out of sight. A red ember of light glowed from the reflector. Checking that the road was clear he stood up in the ditch and pulled the damp parts of his trousers from where they had stuck to his skin. His eye caught the insect which had crossed his hand and he put his foot on it and swivelled it slowly from side to side.

He clambered up the bank. The road felt hard under his feet. Thick hedgerows laced with honeysuckle and hawthorn bound each side of it. He picked up a stone and held it tightly in his hand, its cold hardness giving him a spur of comfort. He would go home now. Staying close to the safety of the ditch he made his way along the road, his senses raw and primed.

Through gaps in the hedge cows stared out at him, their curious eyes deep pools of liquid. One stuck its head between the strands of wire and pulled at grass on the bank, while others followed his path, shadowy shapes behind a screen. Above him trees locked their branches and as he looked up they seemed like a web about to fall. Suddenly something burst from the mesh of leaf and branch and he flung his arm across his face and dropped to the ground, his heart skimming waves of fear. The magpie winged its way across the fields in a flapping flag of black and white. He stood up and walked quickly on, his hand still clutching the stone.

He reached the barley field and stopped at the gate where his father had tied plastic bags to frighten the crows. They fluttered lifelessly like tired balloons. The forgotten scarecrow lurched drunkenly to one side, its arms stretched out in a helpless gesture of submission and its tattered clothes blown ragged by the wind. There were some crows in the field, black smudges against the yellow. He climbed on to the gate and holding the top bar with one hand, threw the stone in their direction. It fell hopelessly short, disappearing into the barley like a stone into water, but it sent the crows funnelling skywards like black smoke, their loud squawks plucking the air. He knew they would come back when he had gone, but it did not matter. Who would harvest it now? He climbed down and continued on, his hand missing the strength of the stone.

He had not gone far when he crouched and listened. Somewhere on the road ahead was a car. Its sound sent a surge of panic through him. On either side unbroken hedgerows fenced him in. He looked behind, but the gate into the barley field was too far away and the ditch had disappeared. They were coming. They were coming back. He was trapped. He bounced from hedgerow to hedgerow before he saw a tiny chink at the foot of the hedge and in desperation forced himself into the gap. Thorns scratched his head and pulled at his clothes but he pushed on, indifferent to the pain. He had almost worked himself clear and into the barley field when he felt himself caught on the branches of hawthorn. He pulled and squirmed but could not break free. The car was almost on him, the noise of its engine roaring in his ears. Shivering with fear he lay face down and covered his ears with his hands, pushing so tightly it was as if he had cupped huge shells over them. When he took them away there was only a ringing silence. The car had gone. He turned and freed his jumper from the thorns – it was badly plucked. Then, still on his front he wriggled free of the hedge and into the cover of the barley field.

He felt cold and sick, and the field quivered in front of him like a great quilted bed, inviting him to snuggle into its hidden folds. Defying one of the rules of the farm, he crawled towards the centre of the field, his body pushing down a track through the stalks. Sometimes he paused and tried to straighten them behind him in an effort to conceal his track. When he felt he had reached the very heart of the field he lay on his side with his arm under his head like a pillow and his knees pulled into his chest. He had stopped shivering now and he imagined the weak, watery sun beginning to warm his body as he rocked himself, the enveloping safety of the sanctuary lulling him into a fitful calm. Around him the wind swirled the barley, unravelling delicate traceries which whispered gently. He fell into a shallow sleep and did not dream.

When he woke he stared at the sky. It seemed close enough to touch. He pushed a hand towards a passing cloud. A gull sliced through the air. There was a funny taste in his mouth and his arm was sore. His hands still carried the red scratches of the thorns and there were ears of seed speckling his woollen jumper. He stood up and brushed them off on to the flattened bed his body had made. His bladder felt tight and full and he urinated over the trampled barley, causing little puffs of steam to shoot up sharply. When he had finished he walked back along the path he had made, his hands plucking roughly at the heads of stalks and shredding the seed between his finger and thumb.

He took the long way back, as always keeping well away

from the big field. He skirted widely round it then left the road to cross the meadow where cow pats hardened in the strengthening sun and fine veils of midges shimmered about his head. Reaching the stream he knelt down and pushed his hand against the current, letting the cold water foam about his fingers. He spat and watched it float away. The water's edge was pock-marked with the hoof prints of cows. He wondered where the herd was now. The slaughterhouse and the butcher's knife. He thought of their yellow-skinned carcases hanging from shiny metal hooks, tiny drops of blood dripping on to sawdust floors. He imagined their blood flowing into the stream, turning it red, then snatched his hand out of the water and wiped it repeatedly across his trousers. Stepping carefully on the flat stones he crossed the stream and started to run. In the corner of the field he saw a rabbit, its fur discoloured and slimy, and when it started away to shelter it moved slowly and without urgency.

As he climbed to the high end of the meadow he could see the farm buildings nestling in the hollow below. Grey wisps of smoke were coming from the chimney and above it spurts of swallows stitched the sky with sharp twists of black. The first pair had arrived a month earlier and had relined their old nest which cradled under the eaves of the barn. Then others had come. His father had said they did no harm and would only stay a short while. Once when they had been walking together they had stopped and watched their acrobatic flight. Now they wreathed the house. Soon they too would be gone, their nests under eaves and rafters the only reminders of their presence.

There were two cars in the yard. People came to the

house most days. He knew one belonged to their pastor and one to his uncle and aunt. When he touched the bonnets of the cars they were still warm. He wondered how long they would stay. Turning the handle of the kitchen door slowly and gently, he opened it just wide enough to let himself squeeze through. In the kitchen the tap dripped sullenly and the biscuit tin sat open. In the sink slumped two tea bags. A growing pile of unopened tins was stacked in one corner – each time someone called they brought something they had baked. The fridge hummed steadily and the stove gave a tiny creak. A petal fell from the wilting geranium on the window-sill and fluttered on to the work top. He could hear their voices in the living-room. The door was partially closed and he was able to drift by it and reach the stairs without being seen. With the advantage of intimacy he picked his steps carefully, placing his feet where he knew they would produce no creak or noise, and made his way to the top stair. He rested his head in his hands, then perched motionless. He could hear the pastor's slow voice.

'It's no easy road you're travelling on now Elizabeth. It's a hard way the Lord has chosen for you but I believe the Lord never sends us affliction but he gives us the grace to bear it. In my own life I've found it to be so. If we put all our faith in Him we can draw on His strength to see us through. That's what you must do now Elizabeth, cleave unto Him, and hold nothing back. None of us may understand now why this terrible thing has happened but one day when the light of the Holy Spirit illuminates our sight we shall see the Divine purpose behind it.'

'It's hard Pastor, it's very hard.' His mother's voice

sounded wavering and fragile. 'He never did any harm
to anyone – it wasn't in him to harm a living soul and
look what they did to him. Cut him down as if he was
some sort of animal.'

He could hear her sobs of pain and bitterness, drawn
from a deep well which seemed incapable of running dry.
His aunt was comforting her, talking to her the way she
might have spoken to a child, consoling, hushing, gently
scolding. He put his hands over his ears and screwed his
eyes tightly closed, but he could not block out the sobs.
It was as if they came from inside him.

'What sort of people are they Pastor that can do these
things?' his mother asked, sounding like a child asking an
adult to explain some terrible mystery.

'They're not people at all who can do the likes of
that,' protested his uncle angrily.

'The Bible says the heart of man is exceedingly wicked,'
the Pastor replied. 'There's a spirit of evil loose in this land
and the Devil has no shortage of willing workers. But
there's one thing we should all be mindful of and that
is one day these men with their blood-stained hands will
have to give an account of their deeds. It might not be
in the courts of this land, or even in our lifetime, but
one day they'll stand before their Maker and the judgement
throne, and answer for what they've done.'

'It's more than those two who have something to
answer for,' his uncle continued, unappeased. 'There were
others who put the finger on Tom, locals, maybe even
neighbours, and they're as guilty as the ones who pulled
the trigger.'

'That's why it's best to move away,' said his aunt.

7

'How could Elizabeth live here and look at people and all the time be wondering if they were the ones? Better to make a new start somewhere fresh. And at least now the Sandfords have bought the farm it means it'll not pass into the wrong hands.'

There was silence for a few seconds. A cup chinked against a saucer. He hoped they would go soon.

'Then there's Samuel to think of,' his aunt continued. 'Better for him to start somewhere new, somewhere he won't see things every day to remind him. A new school in September, new friends – it's for the best.'

'And Samuel . . . how is Samuel, Elizabeth?' asked the pastor, his voice edged with caution.

'Much the same, much the same,' she gasped, her strength ebbing with each word.

'A terrible thing for any human soul to see but for a boy . . . his own father . . . It's a terrible thing – there's no two ways about it,' the Pastor said.

'And is he still . . . ? In the night, Elizabeth?' his aunt asked.

There was no spoken answer.

'It'll pass Elizabeth,' his uncle affirmed. 'I know it's hard to believe but he's a growing boy and he's a tough boy. He'll come through it, he'll come through the other side. It just needs time.'

'You've got to be strong for him,' urged his aunt. 'He needs you more than ever now and there's not an hour of the day when the Lord's family isn't praying that you will receive the strength to cope.'

'But I don't feel strong,' his mother whimpered. 'I feel like I just want to lie down somewhere and die.

Forgive me Pastor but I just don't think I can see this thing through.'

She was crying again and there was the sound of moving chairs. He stood up and peered over the banisters but could only see a few feet into the room. Sitting down again he stared at the angry red scrapes on his hands then licked his tongue along their ridged lengths. There were still flecks of seed on his clothing and he picked them off, letting them float to the bottom of the stairs. Then he heard the pastor saying that they would pray and he knew the visit was coming to a close. Without being able to see he knew they would be kneeling on the floor, elbows resting on their chairs, hands tightly clasped, and faces lined with concentration. As the booming voice forced its way into the silent corners of the house he turned away and entered his bedroom.

'And as Father we bring before You this grieving family we beseech Your Holy Spirit to minister unto them in this their hour of deepest need.'

He crouched down in the tight space between the wardrobe and the wall. Above his bed he could see bright squares on the wallpaper where once pictures had been stuck, and the dried-up crinkled bits of Sellotape which had held them.

'Give them the grace and strength to bear their heavy burden. Take away this thorned crown and let them know Thy peace, which is the peace which passeth all understanding.'

A tea-chest sat in the middle of the floor. There were still some small leaves of tea in the paper at the bottom. He had seen them when he was packing his books and possessions. All around stretched the patterned wallpaper where a hundred faces lurked, to emerge each night in the twilight world before sleep.

'Guide them through the difficult days that lie ahead and bless Elizabeth as she seeks to make a new home in the city. Be near to Samuel and heal the wounds which now afflict his soul.'

A swallow hurtled towards the window then looped back on itself in a black pulse of speed. Others followed it, darting into pockets of space.

'We think too, O Lord, of our province at this dangerous time when each day there is more shedding of innocent blood. We feel that we are a people besieged in our own land and we ask that You may smite the enemy at our gate. The forces of government and state have deserted us and, in this our hour of need, we turn to You for our succour and deliverance. Pour down Your wrath on those who daily sow the seeds of death and destruction and confound their evil schemes. Finally, our Father, we ask You to support Your children with Thy everlasting arms, fill them with Thy Holy Spirit, and above all give them the strength to say like Thy servant of old, "The Lord giveth and the Lord taketh away, blessed be the name of the Lord".'

He put his hand to the bottom of the wardrobe door and flapped it back towards him so that it walled in his narrow little space, darkening and sealing it. He pulled his knees up tightly until only the tips of his whitened shoes were visible and shut his ears against the words, heard only the strange whisperings of his heart. He shut his ears against the words, heard only the whispering voice telling him to block out the screams, to hide in silence, wear it like a coat buttoned tight about his being. Grow small and safe, locked deep inside himself, small and safe like a silent stone in the ditch.

HE RAISED THE edge of the net curtain with the back of his fingers and peered into the street. A man who had got out of the van parked outside the house next door was screwing a SOLD sign onto the bottom of the estate agent's board. Rain was beginning to fall and sullen clouds loomed overhead, darkening the afternoon. He was a young man with blond hair, dressed in a white T-shirt and jeans, and he seemed to be in a hurry to get the job done. When he had finished attaching the SOLD sign, he straightened the post, which had been blown askew in the winter months of wind and storm, by hammering a wedge into the ground. The garden itself had grown wild through neglect, with weeds overwhelming the flower beds and the grass sprouting tall and ragged. The straggly privet hedge sagged in places where children had pushed each other into it, and in mildewed corners roses spurted sickly colours and dropped blackened petals into the wilderness which tangled about their roots.

When the young man had finished his task he hurried

off, letting the gate swing loudly behind him. He watched the van until it disappeared. The rain was heavier now and thick low clouds seemed to flatten out the lingering brightness of the day. Weighted drops splashed the window and raced into nothingness. He let the curtain fall and walked back to the table. He would come soon. He had waited a long time but it was almost over. It was nearly time. Soon he would come. He went back to the white-clothed table. In the middle of it sat a pile of identical green-backed ledgers. Edges of newspaper cuttings peeped out of them. Picking up the top one he slowly turned the pages, pausing as he studied each one, his mouth silently forming the words which his finger underlined. Sometimes he pushed his face close to the photographs as if lodging them deep in his memory. His hands delicately smoothed wrinkles and traced over the pages as if they were written in braille. Then, reaching some page deep in the ledger, he stopped and closed his eyes, his hands gripping the edges of the table for support. When he opened his eyes again he read the page deliberately, as if forcing himself to finish it. When he had done so, he sat back and glanced towards the window. It was still raining.

He continued turning the pages of the ledger until he reached the end of the cuttings. Two clean white pages stared up at him. He went to the sideboard where newspapers were stacked in neat piles. He searched through one of the piles until he found the paper he was looking for, and from a drawer took out a small pair of scissors and a pot of paste, then returned to the table. Straightening the paper on the table, he squared it up as if it were a deck of playing cards, then carefully, with his tongue peeping out the corner of his mouth, cut out the photograph on the front and pasted it onto the blank page. He had put too much glue on and some oozed out the sides. Taking his handkerchief, he dabbed at it until the excess had been soaked up, then sat back and studied it. He looked mainly at the boy, scanning his features, touching him gently with the tips of his fingers as if absorbing him through touch. Soon he would come. The wait was nearly over. He smoothed the photograph one final time with his handkerchief, then read the caption aloud, slowly and carefully.

'THE WIDOW OF MURDERED UDR SERGEANT THOMAS ANDERSON COMFORTS HER TWELVE-YEAR-OLD SON SAMUEL AT THIS MORNING'S FUNERAL.'

Then he closed his eyes, clasped his hands together in front of his bowed head and prayed silently for a long time.

When he had finished he closed the ledger and returned it to the top of the pile, then carried them to the drawer of the sideboard where they were kept. He locked it and placed the key behind the clock which sat in the middle of the fireplace. It had stopped raining and pockets of brightness were beginning to edge out the smothering greyness of the afternoon. He had many things to do and he listed them in his mind. He began by taking the newspaper from the table and spreading it on the tiled hearth, then shovelled the previous night's ashes onto it. He piled a little heap in the middle, then folded over the corners of the paper to make a scrunched-up parcel. Leaving it on the hearth, he took the ash-tray through the kitchen and out the back door to where the dustbin stood. A breeze blew ash onto his clothes and a fine film of white layered his hands. As he emptied the ashes into the bin, ash puffed up into the air until he smothered it with the metal lid.

He set down the empty tray, went to the wooden shed and found a hatchet. Its head was loose and he banged the handle on the ground until it was jammed tight then used it to cut sticks, slicing slivers of wood from an assortment of off-cuts and scraps he had gathered. Sometimes the blade struck on a knot and he tapped the ground until it forced through a path. Carrying the sticks in the empty ash-tray, he returned to the fire and placed them on a bed of crumpled paper, then positioned the cinders carefully, mindful not to pile them too deeply in case they smothered the flames. He took the box of matches from the fireplace and tried to strike one, but it broke in two and he dropped it onto the cinders. When the second match sparked into life, his hand shook a little, but he managed to light the corners of the newspaper, holding it until it almost burnt his hand. The fire spread slowly at first then gained a hold and the sticks started to crackle. Placing his face close to the bars of the grate he blew softly, making the flames flicker brightly. Soon all the sticks had caught alight and yellow-tipped flames poked through gaps in the cinders. He rubbed the side of his face with his hand, leaving a grey streak on his cheek.

He sat down on his chair at the side of the fire and watched it closely. Soon he would add a few small pieces of coal from the scuttle, but not just yet. The fire's light forced the final vestiges of gloom from the room. Cinders began to glow gently. He drew strength from its light.

Often he felt the burden of his appointed task, the terrible weight of the work he must do in the face of darkness – so much darkness all around, more than one man could dispel. But he was no longer relying on himself for the bright flame of light – it would be given, if only he had faith, eyes to see, ears to listen. Sometimes he wondered why God had chosen him, picked him alone from all His servants. Like Moses, he had questioned God, doubted his own worthiness, said, 'But behold, they will not believe me, nor hearken unto my voice for they will say, The Lord hath not appeared unto thee.' For a long time he had tried to hide from the knowledge, tried to find reasons why he was the wrong choice.

He lifted down his Bible and opened it at the marker. 'And Moses said unto the Lord, O my Lord I am not eloquent, neither heretofore, nor since thou hast spoken unto Thy servant, but I am slow of speech and of a slow tongue. And the Lord said unto him, Who hath made man's mouth? or who maketh the dumb, or deaf, or the seeing, or the blind? have not I the Lord? Now therefore go, and I will be with thy mouth, and teach thee what thou shalt say.' The understanding of these words had driven away the doubts. He was waiting, his soul ready. Flames poked through the darkness. Soon a bright light of healing would burst through the darkness. Soon it would be time. God had given him the boy. He was finally coming and his heart gave thanks for the gift.

Lifting the tongs from the hearth, he dropped a few pieces of coal among the cinders then set the fireguard in place. It was buckled and jagged ends of wire plucked at his knuckles. Then he went into the kitchen and washed

his hands, having to rub hard at the thin tongue of soap
to produce any lather, and dried them on the faded towel
which hung limply from a rail at the back of the door. He
sat down on one of the two kitchen chairs and reached for
his boots. As he lifted them the heels swung together and
a little crust of dry mud flaked to the floor. He folded
over the toe of his grey woollen sock and squirmed his
foot into the first one then laced it tightly, finishing with
a double knot. When the second was almost on, he stood
up straight and tested that they were securely on by pushing his weight into them and stamping on the spot like a
soldier marking time. He put on his jacket which had been
hanging on the back of the chair and searched aimlessly
in the pockets for a few seconds. The grey mark on his
cheek smouldered like a scar. Then he went out into the
back garden.

All traces of rain had seeped away and a pale yellow
sun hung tremulously in the sky. Only the dampness of
the grass and the droplets of water weighing down the
heads of flowers indicated the heaviness of the earlier
rain. He stopped occasionally to pull the dead head of a
flower, crumpling the petals in his hands and letting them
sprinkle to the ground like confetti. Where the wind had
blown the clump of white-faced daisies he paused to push
them together and straighten the stakes which held them
upright. The grass would need cutting soon. His fingers
felt the scented velvety softness of rose petals and without
knowing why he slipped them into his pocket.

The garage smelt of the rotting grass which stuck
to the roller of the lawnmower. Along two of the
walls makeshift shelves sagged under the weight of tins

of paint, with crusted lids and thick drips striping their sides, assorted bottles of grimy liquid, rusted biscuit tins stacked high with nails, screws, door handles and tools. The brown-ribbed remnants of a threadbare carpet, its faded floral swirls splashed with oil stains, stretched into shadowy corners where rubbish piled up in tiered layers. Across the rafters rested planks of wood, an old door with blistered flaking paint and a bicycle frame. In the rotting corners of the window frames dead flies decayed among dense shrouds of web. Going to the window he pulled the curtains closed, making sure that they left no gap through which unwelcome eyes might pry. Grainy shafts of dust-flecked light fanned through the thin frayed curtains, spearing the gloom.

He checked the door was tightly closed then sat down on a paint-splattered chair which nestled among the accumulation of debris. His eyes flitted nervously, resting briefly on some object before moving on again, exploring with curiosity the discarded remnants of a lifetime. They crossed oil-coated blackened pieces of machinery, deep boxes overflowing with mechanical parts, moss-mottled lengths of guttering, a ladder with broken rungs, and always they circled back towards the same spot. At first he was reluctant to focus on it, almost as if he wanted to disguise his desire to look, to confirm its existence by stealth. A fly buzzed behind the curtain, pinging the glass in its confusion to escape. As he sat straight-backed on the chair, both hands resting on his knees, a thin shaft of light lit up the ash-marked side of his face and dust danced weightlessly to some silent music. Then the sunlight suddenly died and he faded into the half-light, his motionless form drawn imperceptibly into a shadowy world where it blended with the discarded and the forgotten.

He sat for a long time wandering in a world of dream and memory. The fly buzzed more loudly. His gaze turned to an old television set. It was almost completely covered by bits of wood and cardboard boxes. On top of it rested a coiled garden hose and a rolled-up rug. He stood up and walked slowly towards it, hesitated for a second, then began to remove the objects which masked and covered it. He did so carefully, removing them one at a time and setting them down on the floor in a kind of pattern. A spider scurried out from its stolen shelter. When he had cleared them all he turned the set round and looked at the back, then, with shaking fingers, prised it open. In the cleaned-out shell was a green shoe box. He lifted the box level with his chest and carried it back to the chair, holding it tightly in both hands as if afraid that he might drop it. When he had sat down he rested the box on his knees, lifted the lid and let it drop to the ground. Inside was an object wrapped in a yellow oiled cloth and tied up with two black shoe laces. He undid the knots and drew back the corners of the cloth, uncovering the barrel of the gun. His fingers touched its ridged length lightly, then pulled back as if burnt. As he bowed his head over it with closed eyes and mouth working wildly, strange fragmented images filled his head and above them all hovered a dark angel with wings of death. He stretched out his hand into the murky half-light, fingered the blood on the lintels then let his arm fall lifelessly to his side.

His fingers fumbled with the laces, finding it difficult to retie the knots. He glanced at the curtained window and the closed door as he returned the box to its hiding place. Piece by piece, he returned everything as close to its original position as he could remember. When he had finished he stood back and viewed the arrangement. Once or twice he moved something slightly until he was satisfied that nothing looked disturbed or altered. Then he drew back the curtains and light skirmished with the shadows, forcing its way into the narrow gaps between objects and pushing into the webbed crevices of silence. He took one final look, then went out and locked the door behind him.

As he dropped the key into his pocket his fingers felt the softness of the rose petals. He wondered how they had got there. Then the voices told him that the boy had given them to him – given them as a sign of his coming. He stopped and took them out, cupping them as if they were water in the hands of a thirsty man. His eyes stroked their velvety surface, explored their blemished beauty. The boy had given them to him. He counted them, blowing gently into his hands to make sure that none was covered by another. There were six. He counted them again. Six. It was a sign. The boy would come in six days. He lifted his cupped hands slowly to the sky then opened them until the petals scattered in the wind.

HE SAT WITH his mother in the back seat of his uncle's car, having pressed the locking button of the door, and slipped into the softness of the upholstery. His mother sat in her best coat, the white handkerchief which wreathed her hand pulled tight like a bracelet. At the rear of the car his uncle experimented with the suitcases, trying to work out the best arrangement, while his aunt supervised with impatient and exasperated gestures. The slam of the boot made him jump and dig his fingers into the seat. His mother glanced towards him and smiled a tight-lipped reassurance.

'It's for the best, Samuel. We could never manage the farm. It's better for someone to take it over and look after it properly. It's what your father would have wanted.'

He looked up at the windows where the reflections of clouds addled in the glass. In his bedroom the hidden faces in the walls would stare now only into emptiness, the insidious, whispering voices would snake through the husks of rooms and fade into silence. He looked at the

21

heavy front door with its black knocker and letter box, as it squatted solid and secure like the tight lid of a box, and wondered if it would be strong enough to shut in all the evil which sought to lay hold of him and ensnare his being. If it was strong enough he might escape through this journey, escape their clutches and vanish into some safer world where their sharp talons might not reach. If only he could run far enough, run fast enough, he might find some hiding place where their cruel eyes might not seek him out.

'I just feel it's for the best. There's nothing here for us now – only bad memories. We've got to look forward and try to make a new home. You and me together in a new home.'

She nodded her head and slowly transferred the handkerchief from one hand to the other, then turned her face away from him and looked out of the window. He stared at the back of her head. The sunlight coming through the rear window of the car lit up her hair, little wisps of grey veining the brown.

As the car set off slowly down the long lane to the road, his uncle and aunt talked incessantly as if frightened of drowning in the deep pool of silence which had formed round their departure. His mother seemed lost in her memories and kept her face angled to the window, while he peered out at the world he had known and wished his uncle would drive faster. Some swallows plummeted – dark drops of speed – then looped back on themselves. Soon, they, too would leave. Empty nests under eaves. A long line of hedgerow unravelled past his window, so close that he could have reached out and touched it. Its deep pockets of mottled leaf and branch were riddled with blossom and its roots vanished into thick verges where the grass grew tall and wild. He searched it constantly for watching faces or camouflaged shapes screened behind the secret veil of hedge. He sank a little lower in the seat until his eyes were level with the bottom of the glass.

'Are you looking forward to being a city boy, Samuel?' his aunt asked, turning her head slightly towards him.

The hedgerow vanished and was replaced by a stone wall, its surface weathered with whorls of yellow and white, while bearded ferns fanned around the base of the stones.

'Yes, he's looking forward to it,' his mother replied. 'There's a lot more life in the city than the country, lots more things to do.'

'It'll take a while to get used to it,' said his uncle as he increased the speed of the car. 'But young people can adapt to things a lot more easily than us older ones. Isn't that right, Samuel?'

He met his uncle's eyes in the mirror for a second, then looked away. They were reaching the end of the lane. He could hear strange noises in his head. He closed his eyes and held tightly onto the armrest. The door of the house was beginning to creak. Suddenly, a lightning-shaped crack splintered the wood and shot deep forks into the grain. It bulged forward, groaning under the black weight pounding behind it until screws popped out and it sagged forward then ripped open like the flailing skin of a drum. Windows shattered in a tinkling eruption of glass and curtains streamed into the yard like fluttering

23

banners. They were coming! They were coming! He had been foolish to think that they would let him go so easily. He looked into the wing mirror of the car but he knew already that they could not be seen – they could not be seen and could not be touched, but they were always there. He closed his eyes and shrank far into himself.

'You've always been a bit of a townie at heart, Elizabeth,' his aunt said.

'I suppose you're right, Joan. I like the country all right, but I think it takes you to be born in it to really feel you belong.'

She turned her face into the car and smiled a little.

'Do you remember when we were just married? I cried my eyes out I was so homesick. It's a wonder Tom didn't pack my bags and send me straight home to my mother.'

Then the smile faded slowly and she turned her head away again.

'I mind it well enough,' replied his uncle. 'And what about that first Christmas when you insisted on dragging him all the way up to Belfast to do your shopping. We all thought he'd married a right Lady Muck.'

His mother laughed a little at the memory and as the car reached the village she rocked herself gently with a warm, lulling song of the past. People going about their shopping stopped and waved to them. They passed the church with its winding gravel driveway; the cluster of tiny shops; the public house with its green glass windows and window boxes. Leaving the main street, they found themselves stuck behind a tractor pulling a trailer, but eventually the familiar was left behind as the car sped on its way to their new life. Country roads gave way to main roads and then, in time, to the motorway. But never fast enough, never fast enough to leave his pursuers behind. They winged their steady way, watching and following with the insistent flapping of tireless wings.

Along the side of the motorway crows pecked at empty cigarette packets and magpies scrambled across crash barriers to rest in white-barked trees. Long lorries hurtled by, making the car feel small and vulnerable and at times steep banks of grass channelled them to their destination. The further they drove from their old home, the more his mother's thoughts turned to the future. She talked as if trying to convince herself that everything would work out well but occasionally little moments of doubt appeared.

'I'm sure Belfast's changed since I was a girl. There's been a lot of redevelopment, a lot of the old streets knocked down. And even the centre of Belfast – I hardly recognized it the last time we were there. It's all new shops and big stores. Very nice, like, but different from when we were young.'

'There's lots of changes all right,' his aunt agreed. 'Do you remember when we used to go every Saturday afternoon and spend the few bob we had gathered up between us over the week? Do you mind the times we used to make a cup of tea last an hour in Marshalls?'

The conversation slipped once more into the past. His mother seemed increasingly drawn into the safe world of days long gone, almost as if she hoped that by going far enough back, she might be able to return to the present by a different road. The motorway reached the outskirts of Belfast. From his window he could see playing fields and houses, and beyond them the Lough burrowing its way into the mouth of the city. Through his mother's window tiers of houses spread up the slopes of the black ridged mountain. Then the motorway merged with more lanes and drew them closer to the city. In the distance he could see yellow cranes perched at the waterside like birds about to dip their heads. They passed through a tunnel of blue-badged bridges and tall T-shaped lights into a nowhere world littered with the backs of factories and warehouses, wedges of land planted with young trees and shrubs. A train crawled along past rows of terraced houses. Spider writing moved across grey gable walls.

'Over there's the York Road where your grandmother lived, Samuel,' his mother said, pointing her wreathed hand. 'She had a grocer's shop on the corner of Alexandra Park Avenue. And that train reminds me of going to Portrush for our Sunday School excursions. Those were good times – a day out on the train then was a real adventure.'

'Aye, a few sandwiches and a bag of buns and we were as happy as sandboys,' his uncle said. 'Do you recall the sports on the beach? Egg and spoon races, sack races – the whole works.'

'Mind the time me and Elizabeth won the three-legged race?' asked his aunt, laughing. 'Betty Donaldson and her cousin were raging because they'd been practising for weeks. They tripped just after the start and she ripped her best dress.'

'That's right,' his mother remembered excitedly, 'and we each got a bar of white chocolate.'

He listened to their gentle laughter. Seagulls hovered above a refuse dump.

'Listen,' urged his uncle, 'why don't we all take a drive up the Antrim Coast and go to Portrush? In a couple of weeks when you're settled in? What do you say, Samuel?'

His mother touched him lightly on his leg and smiled at him. His uncle's eyes watched him in the driver's mirror. He met them briefly, then nodded his head. A yellow bulldozer was pushing refuse into a pit.

'That's good, that's good. I don't think these two girls are up to three-legged races anymore, but we could have a good day out. And look, quick! There's Seaview where the Crues play. Many's a match I used to watch there. Their nickname was "The Hatchet Men" – no fancy Dans in those days. Some Saturdays the ball was more often on the railway line.'

Spider writing moved across more walls but the car was travelling too quickly for it to speak to him. They left the motorway and followed a road round the outskirts of the city centre, past the docks where a ferry boat suddenly reared up its blue funnels like chimneys, and then through the Markets area. As the car headed across the city he grew nervous again. So many faces – more than he could register or scan. They surged on the pavements and peered out at him from the shadows of doorways. Like the hidden faces in his room they stared down at him and there were too many to hide from. They swarmed about the car, searching him out and whispering to each other. Neon shop signs pointed him out and although he sank lower in the seat he could still feel their penetrating gaze and hear tongues rustling like the wind moving dead leaves. Two men stepped off the pavement so close to the car that they might have reached out and opened the door. Their eyes were sharp slits of hate. Black taxis shuttled alongside the car, their insides filled to overflowing. His mother had grown quiet and still.

Gradually they moved into the suburbs in the southeast of the city. His uncle told him it would not be long. The car turned off the main road and began to climb the winding avenues. A woman struggled to push a pram up the steepness with two small children holding on to the tail of her coat.

'It'll be good exercise walking up here,' his uncle joked. 'Put a few muscles on your legs.'

They turned into a tree-lined avenue where the houses were only distinguishable from each other by the colour of paintwork or the quality of garden. It seemed a quiet, sleepy sort of place and there were few people about. A few cars sat parked in driveways and tall privet hedges protected many of the fronts from prying eyes, while behind the houses narrow strips of garden stretched up the sharp slope of the hillside.

As his uncle parked the car across the driveway of their new home he peered up at the house. The windows stared back betraying no trace of what lay beyond. The SOLD sign moved slightly in the rising breeze. His mother seemed suddenly gripped by doubt and made no move to get out of the car. His uncle began to unload the cases, hoping to generate some enthusiasm through his display of energy, while his aunt fumbled for something in her handbag. Slowly his mother opened her door, got out and stood looking up at the house. She smoothed her hair nervously, then stretched her hand out towards him, signalling him to accompany her. He followed a few paces behind as she opened the gate and inspected the tiny mess of garden.

'Give us something to do,' she said. 'We'll soon have it in shape.'

The key wouldn't turn in the lock and as his mother struggled with it he stood close behind her. She took the key out, looked at it, then tried again. This time it turned and she pushed open the door for him to enter. He stepped cautiously into the silent hall, then hesitated by the foot of the stairs, his senses searching the sounds and smells, sifting through their strangeness for signs of danger. He took it all in – the wooden banisters faded and smoothed by the touch of many hands, a brown carpet with a yellow-flowered pattern, cream painted doors with grey metal handles and black scuff-marks at the bottom. His hand felt the textured surface of the white and gold embossed wallpaper. A white metal glass-topped telephone table jutted out from the wall. The draught from the open door moved the bowl-shaped lamp shade very slightly. Through the kitchen he could see blue formica work tops, the window and the garden beyond. A stillness held the house fast, uncertain, weightless, undefined.

'Go on, it won't bite you.'

His mother touched him gently on the back. He walked down the hall, his fingers lightly skimming the closest wall. Looking into the front sitting-room, he recognized their furniture from home.

'Doesn't it look well?' his mother asked, her voice flecked with pride.

He nodded his head and then walked into the living-room. His mother followed and opened the windows before going into the kitchen and filling the kettle. His uncle carried the suitcases into the hall. It was smaller than their room at home but the familiar furniture did nothing to make the room less strange. All around him were furniture and ornaments which had been brought from the farm but they looked anxious and ill-at-ease. Familiar photographs hung on strange walls, chairs sat at awkward angles to each other. The whole house seemed like a man wearing someone else's ill-fitting clothes.

'Go up and look at your room. Your things are in the front room – the one with the view.'

His aunt and uncle were sitting on stools in the kitchen, opening tins and looking for spoons. He let his hand slide along the rounded smoothness of the banister and climbed the stairs, feeling the muffled looseness of the carpet beneath his feet. The stairs were shorter and less steep than those at home. In the room squatted the tea-chests with his unpacked belongings but he walked past them and stared down into the city below. That night before sleep, he stared down once again, searched the deep trough of blackness where amber lights glowed – a great trough scooped out between the hills and beaded with amber. And as he stood he could hear their mocking laughter, and though he clasped his hands to his ears, it burst out loud and fierce, and he knew that nothing had changed.

ACTS OF CONSECRATION
TO THE
IMMACULATE HEART OF MARY

(for Religious and Laity)
(Longer Form)

Virgin of Fatima, Mother of Mercy, Queen of Heaven and Earth, Refuge of Sinners, we who belong to the Marian Movement consecrate ourselves in a very special way to your Immaculate Heart.

By this act of consecration we intend to live, with You and through You, all the obligations assumed by our baptismal consecration. We further pledge to bring about in ourselves that interior conversion so urgently demanded by the Gospel, a conversion that will free us of every attachment to ourselves and to easy compromises with the world so that, like You, we may be available only to do always the will of the Father.

And as we resolve to entrust to you, O Mother most sweet and merciful, our life and vocation as christians, that You may dispose of it according to your designs of salvation in this hour of decision that weighs upon the world, we pledge to live it according to your desires especially as it pertains to a renewed spirit of prayer and penance, the fervent participation in the celebration of the Eucharist and in the works of the apostolate, the daily recitation of the Holy Rosary, and an austere manner of life in keeping with the Gospel, that shall be to all a good example of the observance of the law of God and the practice of the christian virtues, especially that of purity.

We further promise You to be united with the Holy Father, with the Hierarchy and with our Priests, in order to thus set up a barrier to the growing confrontation directed against the Magisterium, that threatens the very foundation of the Church.

Under your protection, we want to be apostles of this sorely needed unity of prayer and love for the Pope, on whom we invoke your special protection.

And lastly, insofar as is possible, we promise to lead those souls with whom we come in contact to a renewed devotion to You.

Mindful that atheism has caused shipwreck in the faith to a great number of the faithful, that desecration has entered into the Holy Temple of God, and that evil and sin are spreading more and more throughout the world, we make so bold as to lift our eyes trustingly to You, O Mother of Jesus and our merciful and powerful Mother, and we invoke again today and await from You the salvation of all your children, O clement, O loving, O sweet Virgin Mary. (with ecclesiastical approval)

Printed by C.P.S. Tel 042 40417

HE HAD FINALLY come. He watched from his kitchen window as the boy explored the garden and shed. He was smaller than he had imagined and his hair was red, rather than the brown colour the newspaper photograph had suggested. He gave a little prayer of thanks. Already the burden of the work which lay ahead felt lighter; God had sent him a helpmate and soon He would reveal the plan that He wished them both to carry out – the plan that would send His holy light to vanquish the darkness, bring healing to the sick and the dying.

He watched the boy intently, absorbing his every movement, anxious to miss nothing. He felt frustrated as the boy disappeared inside the shed, impatient at the time he spent out of view. Part of him wished to go straight to him but he knew he must be careful, listen to the guiding voice which pulsed in his head. A few minutes later the boy emerged and closed the shed door behind him, then studied the straggle of shrubs and trees which bordered the bottom of the garden. Beyond the back fence a field of tussocky grass swept upwards into the overlooking hills. When the boy turned and came back towards the house he saw his face clearly for the first time. His eyes narrowed in concentration as he took in the boy's features, committing them to memory. As he came closer he watched his light-coloured eyes flit nervously from side to side, saw a small pale moon of a face stippled with freckles and red hair which got redder as the light hit it. He moved to the side of the kitchen curtain so that the boy would not see him.

Just then the front door of the house opened and he heard loud laughter. He pulled back from the curtain and started to fill the kettle, but he turned the tap on too hard and the water splashed off its rim and sprayed onto the boards. Some of it splashed onto his clothes.

'All right, Da? Trying to start another flood?'

He made no answer but brushed the droplets off with the palms of his hands, then reached for the dishcloth and dried the boards.

'If you're putting the kettle on, make Cindy and me a cup. I've a throat like a sandpit. Traipsin' round the town'd put years on you. It's not fit work for any man.'

'If you like, Mr Ellison, I'll do it,' the girl said, smiling up at him and reaching out to take the kettle. He pulled it away from her hand.

'I can make a cup of tea,' he said.

'Come on, Dad, don't start. Cindy's only trying to be helpful. Let her make the tea.'

Reluctantly, he handed over the kettle and she patted him on the arm as she might have a child. He sat down

at the kitchen table and stared at the blue chequered
cloth.

'Billy, do you want one of these buns we bought,
or do you want to keep it for later?'

'Ah, give us it now. Who knows, we might all be
dead later on. And give ma da one as well – keep him
happy.'

At his son's words he turned his head away and looked at
the wall. A fine crack ran down the plaster then broke into
a rush of tributaries. His son took off his leather jacket and
hung it over the back of the chair, its metal zips bristling
coldly.

'Well, what've you been getting up to today, Dad?'
he said, winking at the girl. 'Out saving the world from
eternal damnation?'

'Don't mock God's work. God is not mocked. Why
do you always scorn what is precious?'

'Sorry, Dad,' he said as he loosened the laces of his
trainers. 'No messing, what've you been doing?'

'I've been working in the garden, getting things ready.'

'Right, the garden . . . good. Don't go overdoing
things, though – I don't want you laid up with a bad
back. I've better things to do with my time than waiting
hand and foot on you.'

'Have you, William? What better things have you to
do with your time? Tell me, son,' he said, looking into
his son's eyes.

'You know already, Dad. What are you asking again
for? I scrape a living. I get by. And anyway, it's not as
if I go around asking you for money.'

'But I don't know. And that's always worried me.'

33

'Give it a break, Da, give it a break.'

'Come on you two, the tea's almost ready. Don't be fighting, now – you're worse than children.'

She shook the blond sweep of curls from her face and set the table, her wrist jangling with jewellery. She set it precisely and self-consciously, like a child determined to do it properly under the supervision of a parent, then she served him the bun on a saucer.

'There you go, Mr Ellison – get tore into that. That'll soon make you feel better.'

He glanced up at her, took in her bright red lips and the mass of dyed blond hair which tumbled about one side of her face. Why did she always paint herself? Why did her clothes always reveal so much of her shape? It wasn't seemly for a woman to dress that way. He turned his head away, ashamed.

'Are you not having one?' his son asked her.

'Me? No, sure don't I have to mind my figure,' she said, giggling in the way that always made her sound like a child.

'What figure?' he asked, pushing the first half of the bun into his mouth.

She flicked him playfully on the shoulder then poured the tea, her mouth open with concentration. There were only two chairs so she stood at the sink holding the cup in both hands and looking into the garden. Sometimes a snatch of song slipped from her mouth and she moved her feet in a little shuffle of a dance.

'Your new neighbours have arrived, then. You never said.'

'Have they, Dad?' his son asked, standing up and

staring into the next door garden. 'Right enough – there's the boy.'

He put his arm across the shoulders of the girl and wiped his mouth with the back of his hand.

'There's not much to him,' he said. 'Blink and you'd miss him.'

'Leave him alone, Billy. Poor wee thing. It must've been awful for him. He is very pale looking, though.'

'Looks like a little ghost, apart from that red hair. Poor bugger – he'll not forget what he saw too easily. What do you think, Da?'

'Come away from the window. Leave the child alone – don't let him see you staring at him, like you're gawking at something in the zoo. The boy will be all right. In time, he will be all right.'

'Sure, he's not the first and he won't be the last,' his son said, draining the last dregs from his cup. 'And the boys that done it are still walking about out there laughing about it.'

'There's a day of judgement coming, coming for them and for all of us.'

'It's not coming quickly enough for the boys that done that.'

'It's for God to punish.'

'It's all right you saying that, but these scum have been doing just that and getting away with it for as long as I can remember.'

'Billy's right, Mr Ellison. But let's not fight about it. Life's too short to be always arguing and fighting. Maybe these new people'll be a bit of company for you. Maybe they'll be nice.'

He turned his face away and ran his fingers along the cracks in the wall.

'Come on, Cindy, let's sit next door and look at what you've spent my money on,' his son said, the serious tone of his voice replaced by the familiar ring of casual indifference.

'Wait till I clean up here. It'll only take a few minutes.'

'Leave it, you can do it later.' His voice was insistent and she followed him submissively.

He rose and stared into the garden, but the boy had vanished. He refilled the kettle and began to wash the cups. On the girl's cup was a tiny smudge of lipstick. He scrubbed it with the dishcloth until it was gone. From the living-room came the sound of laughter and bantering argument. Their words flitted in and out of his consciousness. Music began to play. He felt their presence had frightened off the boy, sent him into the shelter of the house. They did not understand. They did not understand anything about the boy. He laid the washed cups and saucers upside down on the draining board. Their voices and the music faded in and out of a crackling static like someone tuning a radio along a waveband. They grew louder and he longed to silence them. The water gurgled down the sink in a throaty roar. Music and voices pounded in his ears and he covered them with his hands but the girl's high-pitched laughter splintered his senses. She was laughing at him, like all the others.

He knew they would go soon. Mostly they only stayed long enough to rest and get ready to go somewhere else. Sometimes he didn't see his son for days at a time. The boy had always loved his own secrets, his own mystery.

Friends, places, possessions – he had always guarded them closely as if sharing them might mean their destruction. Now they were strangers to each other. As each year passed, the secrets grew larger until they encompassed whole areas of their lives. Sometimes he watched his son and wondered who he was. The laughter twisted and tightened round his head. Once the boy had run away from home. He had found him in a secret den he had built from bits of wood he had taken from the building site. It had taken him hours to find him, hours of walking the streets, knocking doors, asking people he met. And when he found him, he found a small boy huddled in the corner of a makeshift den who told him that he wanted to stay there for ever.

He had failed with the boy, failed in every way, and he could not shirk from that knowledge or escape from its wounding pain. The knowledge gnawed away at him, a thorn in his side he must bear to the end of his days. When he thought about it he wondered where it had gone wrong, but he could trawl no answer from the depths of his memories. He had tried to bring the boy up in the right way but he had turned his back on God, followed his own road, and now exulted in his own waywardness. It was a deep trouble to him. What his son did was an abomination before God and one day they must both suffer for it. Now they talked more with silence, terrible silences which seared his soul. He remembered it first when they returned to the empty house after the funeral. And when eventually they spoke, their voices had echoed in the crushing emptiness.

Words seeped slowly from the edges of his memory

like wisps of smoke, and drifted across his mind. Bitter words. Sharp as knives. He tried to shut them out but the laughter burst into a scornful crescendo. And yet he knew too that soon the laughter would cease, for despite his son's transgressions and all his own personal inadequacies, God had chosen him to be the instrument of His will. Why this should be was a mystery which he no longer sought to understand because the ways of God were far beyond the minds of men. What God required of him was not understanding but unquenchable faith and obedience to His voice. If he had harboured lingering doubts, the arrival of the boy dispelled their last traces. The boy had come just as God had promised. Soon it would be time. Their moment drew closer every day. He did not know yet how God would use him to save the sick and the dying, but he did know that it too would be revealed if he had eyes to see and ears to hear. He must still his soul and be ready to hear no other voices but the still, small voice of God.

FROM HIS BEDROOM window he watched the two men get out of their car. They were dressed in dark suits and one wore a dog-collar. They were checking the number of the house against a piece of paper. As the minister stood looking towards the front door he smoothed the wrinkles out of his jacket, while the man who had been driving checked carefully that all the car doors were locked. They both looked hesitant and nervous but there was something official about their appearance. The minister glanced up at the bedroom window and smiled at him, but he stepped back into the room and waited for the sound of the bell. It rang twice before his mother scurried down the hall and opened the door, then with an instinctive lightness of step he moved to the landing and listened to the voices which filtered into the silence, disturbing the little cloud of stillness which had settled over the house.

He missed the first few words of the introductions, but one man was a colonel and the other some sort of army chaplain. They were both English and their accents sounded high and strange, belonging to some world in which he had never been. His mother took them into the living-room and he heard her offering them a cup of tea. He moved onto the top stair and crouched close and hard like a knot that someone had pulled tight. The water gushed into the kettle and cups clinked against saucers as his mother clock-worked mechanically in the kitchen, preparing the tea tray. Sometimes he caught a glimpse of her as she opened cupboards near the door. In the living-room, the men spoke to each other in low voices. His mother looked a little flustered and a jerky hand flicked away a wisp of hair which fell across her forehead. Sometimes her hand did it even when there was no hair out of place. When she carried the tray through she glanced up at him and smiled, then rolled her eyes. The little secret message made him feel close to her and although he felt safe where he was, he wanted to help her through the coming moments, and so he bumped noiselessly down the stairs like a child and followed her into the living-room.

Both men stood up and shook his hand. He was too close to them to risk looking into their faces, but he knew they had been at his father's funeral. When they spoke to him he nodded his head, then sat down in a corner of the room while his mother answered their questions on his behalf as she poured the tea.

'Samuel likes to keep his own counsel these days,' she said.

They nodded blandly in return to signal that they understood whatever she said and then they complimented her on how well the house was looking.

'Still a long way to go,' she said jauntily. 'Plenty

of jobs that need doing to keep Samuel and me busy.'

'It must be quite a change for you living in the city,' the chaplain said, balancing his biscuit on the rim of the saucer.

'Well, I was born here, you know. Of course, things have changed a lot, though I suppose it's the same everywhere.'

They both agreed with her as if anxious to concur with everything she said. Occasionally his mother looked towards him and smiled with her eyes. The two men talked in turn, steering the conversation into safe areas, and helping each other out when it lapsed into silence. The colonel had black, shiny hair and an angular face. Sometimes, his left eyelid twitched a little and each time it did he drummed his knee with his index finger. The chaplain was an older, grey-haired man with a plump red face and watery eyes. When he was listening, he angled his head a little to the side, as if to show he was carefully taking in everything that was said, and nodded constantly.

After an appropriate time they gently edged towards the purpose of their visit. It was the colonel who led off, speaking in his clipped tones but trying to sound friendly and personal.

'You're probably wondering why we've called, Mrs Anderson. We've come because we know that these are difficult times for you and your family and we know how easy it is after – after things have moved on a little to think that you've been forgotten about. And also to offer any practical help that we can, or assist with any pressing financial worries that you might have.'

The chaplain angled his head further to the side and

smiled reassuringly at her, as the colonel continued.

'We know that the pain of your loss will endure long after the media attention has faded. And unfortunately we know, too, from other equally painful experiences that very often the bereaved feel their plight is forgotten by the very society their husbands sought to serve.'

His mother stared impassively forward and said nothing.

'We feel it's important in situations like these that those who have lost husbands or sons do not feel that their sacrifice has been – passed over, or –'

'Or taken lightly,' finished the chaplain. 'Indeed, these are difficult times but you know, as I visit homes which mourn the loss of a loved one, I am struck by the dignity and strength with which they seek to rebuild their lives.'

His watery eyes were fixed on her, but still she said nothing. It was the colonel who spoke.

'Your husband was a very brave man, and I know from everyone I've spoken with that he was highly respected by all those who served with him. The turnout at the funeral was very impressive and I know he showed the same fine qualities in his private life.'

His mother wreathed her hand with a handkerchief.

'My husband was the very best of men. All he lived for was his family and his church. He did no harm to a living soul and wished no one in the world any ill. And they killed him for it, killed him without a thought or a care and I can't ever forget that or forgive it.'

Both his hands gripped the bottom of his chair and he rocked himself gently, trying to spin an invisible cocoon of silence. He longed to push his palms against his ears to block out the screams rising within him; rock, rock, cradle his soul into sweet fields of forgetfulness, but each new word pulled his senses tighter. Rock, rock . . . block out the screams which were trying to prise him open.

'I know you meant well coming here, but please don't tell me that my husband did not die in vain because I know it's a lie. Thomas died in vain, all right, because it didn't change anything. They keep right on killing and nobody does anything to stop them. The Government doesn't care about men like my husband because if they did, they'd have done something a long time ago.'

She flicked away a wisp of hair which had fallen forward onto her forehead and her knuckles whitened as she squeezed the handkerchief into the palm of her hand.

'Please, Mrs Anderson, don't upset yourself. I understand how you must feel and really, believe me, we didn't come here to upset you or to cause you distress,' said the chaplain, his voice dropping to a whisper.

'I know you didn't, but there's one other thing I want to tell you,' his mother insisted. 'I let the army give Thomas a military funeral out of respect to his wishes, but if it had been my decision alone, we would've laid him to rest in private – buried him quietly and decently without the hypocrisy. All the ceremony and all those words which no one listens to anymore. Too many empty words and condemnations from people who've been saying the same things for twenty years.'

The colonel sat back stiffly on the chair, his face colouring with embarrassment, searching for some avenue of escape.

'I can understand why you feel this way, Mrs Anderson,' persisted the chaplain. 'Sometimes I feel not very different from the way you do – I've walked in too many funeral processions, spoken to too many people suffering in the way your family is, not to have had very similar thoughts.'

'Are our lives worth less than English lives? Do the people sitting in government really care about what happens here to the likes of us?' his mother asked, her voice breaking with bitterness.

'I assure you, Mrs Anderson,' the colonel said, 'that the authorities have the highest regard for the people of this Province, and the loyalty and devotion to their country which has led so many of them to make the ultimate sacrifice, is not something which is taken lightly. And because we're talking here in private, I may say that there are many of us who share your frustrations. There are many people in uniform who would welcome only too readily the opportunity to take these people out of existence. But you know as well as I do, that these decisions rest in the hands of politicians, not in the hands of soldiers.'

His mother stared forlornly into the cup she was holding. He wanted to go to her, but like some animal frightened of breaking cover, he hid deeper in himself. His mother stood up. She had something more to say.

'You were right about feeling forgotten about – we feel it, all right. Two minutes on the headlines and then swept aside by some other bit of news. A couple of days later who even remembered his name? And the people who forget are the lucky ones. We would forget too, but

44

we can't, and we'll remember it every day for the rest of our lives.'

She started to put plates back on the tray. The two men looked at each other and the colonel started to say something but the chaplain cut across him.

'Thank you for the tea, Mrs Anderson. It was good to have this opportunity to meet you and your son. And please remember, if there's any way at all that we can be of any help, don't hesitate to get in touch.'

He handed her a small card but she looked away. He set it gently on the fireplace and then both men said goodbye and made their own way down the hall. His mother followed, and as they left he climbed the stairs to his room to watch them go. He heard her close the front door and carry the tray into the kitchen. Outside, the chaplain stood staring up at the leaden sky while the other man was on his knees on the pavement checking the underside of the car. Then he stood up, unlocked the door and brushed both hands clean.

For the rest of the day his mother cleaned the house with a frantic determination. He helped as best he could, clearing out the fire and vacuuming the hall and stairs. He cleaned places that he knew his mother had cleaned the day before and would clean the next day. When he came back to the living-room he saw that the card had gone. Sometimes his mother sang as she worked, the music synchronising with her mechanical movements as she dusted and polished. At times in her darting, frenetic movements she looked like a little automaton that had been wound too tightly. Not long before bedtime she started to bake, as if afraid to leave any minute of the day unfilled with activity, and when she kissed him goodnight she had a stripe of flour on her cheek.

That night before sleeping he stared down into the black pool where yellow lights criss-crossed the darkness like neon necklaces. Sometimes a light flickered like a candle flame blown by the wind. As he closed the curtains he ran his hands down their join, anxious to make sure there was no chink, no little spy hole through which eyes could peer, then pulled the quilt tightly about him. He no longer read before going to sleep. It did not help and sometimes it got mixed into the dreams and made them worse. His hand fingered the still unfamiliar texture of wallpaper and his eyes searched its pattern for the legion of faces that had lurked in the crevices of his old room, but so far none had emerged. But it gave him no feeling of safety because he knew that they waited somewhere else for him, brooding remorselessly in the shadows and planning the right moment to reach out for him.

Sleep was now the great unpredictable part of his life. Sometimes it was his friend, drowning him in a deep sea of oblivion and carrying him safely through to the morning, but sometimes it deceived him, whispering to him to trust it, to give himself to it, and when he had placed his soul in its hands, it took it greedily and carried him to that place he could not bear to go. He had tried many different things to break its power; focusing his mind on a safe, warm moment of the past, repeating a talismanic word over and over until his mind grew numb and dead, holding a small stone in his hand. Once he had even tried prayer but his words floated away aimlessly like thistledown. At other times he invented a new persona for himself and constructed a safer, better story of his life, painting in details like a child colouring a book.

It carried him now, a little boat tugged by swirling currents, rudderless and drifting into dangerous seas. It steered him through the weak, watery eyes of the chaplain into a chain of caverns where the flapping wings of bats beat in serried flurries and sharp-edged images cut him to the bone. In his dreams he saw the colonel on his knees checking the undercarriage of his car, his mother's face whitened with flour like the face of a ghost. The images washed over him, carrying him deeper into the great echoing chambers of his heart where his mother's words – 'every day for the rest of our lives' – reverberated eternally.

The voyage was always different but the destination never changed. It took him to his father. Tall and strong in his dark blue overalls, bits of grass in his hair after a day of silage cutting. Only the big field left to do and the clear blue skies of a summer's evening stretching still and unbroken. Hedgerows alive with colour and blossom, and everywhere, everywhere, the sweet smell of cut grass. He helped his father with many jobs but he liked this one more than any of them. He liked it because it had a start and a finish and when it was done, and the last bale safely stored it felt as if you had really done something big. Sometimes when the weather was likely to change, his father and his uncles would work through the night, their tractor lights shooting moth-filled shafts of light into darkness. But tonight, on this still summer's evening with the sun slowly sinking red, it was only the two of them. Sometimes when he had promised not to tell his mother, he was allowed to drive the tractor, his father perched behind him in the cab, his hand resting on his shoulder and his eye keeping the steering line straight.

The grass is already cut and raked by the machine into ridged furrows, curving round the field like the graded rings of a giant shell. And everywhere lingers the sweet smell of cut grass, the fresh sap of summer lacing the night. Black smoke belches from the tractor and crows fly overhead, then land in the tractor's wake to search through the freshest swathe. As the sun ignites the tops of the hedgerows on the horizon, his father loads the machine which gathers the cut grass. Soon its long red neck spews grass into the baler, firing it in fiercely like a ceaseless torrent of rain bleeding across the sun. In the glow of the setting sun it looks like a dragon breathing fire. He stands watching it. It seems to fill very quickly and when it can take no more his father stops the tractor and climbs down, taking a minute's rest before he drives the filled baler away.

They must have been waiting for him to get out of the tractor. They must have been standing in the hedgerow, watching and waiting for this moment. They both walk across the ridged furrows of grass, moving steadily, not running. He sees them before his father does, but he looks at them with only slight curiosity. When his father registers them they are close enough for their faces to be seen. In his dreams their faces change so often he no longer remembers what they look like and in his dreams something happens to time. Everything slows and freeze-frames – his father staring and then tightening, shouting at him to run, but his words are strangled in his throat as the first shots hit him in the chest. But no sound from their handguns, only the flapping of the birds' wings as they scatter skyward in a sudden black cloud, as the two men run forward, firing more shots, their feet kicking up grass. Shooting into his father's body as it jerks as if in a fit, and then crumples like a child's on the bed of sharp-spiked stubble. Shooting until the guns are jammed or empty. Only one of them looks at him, and only for a second, looks at him with nothing in his eyes, then they both turn and run to the hedge bounding the road. He falls to his knees beside his father's head, afraid to touch him, and his hand feels the warm blood seeping into the grass. Blood on the grass, red as the setting sun being swallowed by the dark ridge of the horizon. He screams, a raw scream of pain and terror. Screams and screams, until every part of him is locked rigid in it.

The scream was still in his throat when he jerked upright in the bed, his eyes wide and staring. Every day for the rest of his life – eyes with nothing in them, bloodied grass in his father's hair, a black cloud of birds beating across the dying sky. His whole body still shuddered as he felt the warm stream of his urine spread slowly across the plastic sheet.

HE HEARD THE scream. It pierced the silent house like a sudden stab of pain. He knew it was the boy. He stood still and listened – but there was nothing more. A sudden jolt of fear shook him. Perhaps something had happened to him . . . perhaps he had been taken from him. But he calmed himself, rebuking himself for his lack of faith, the constant weakness which left him doubting the fulfilment of the appointed plan. He drifted round the darkened house like a shadow, moving slowly from place to place, fingering familiar objects like signposts on his journey, looking into empty rooms as if searching for some faded memory of the past.

He carried the scream in his head, pondering its meaning, stopping at regular intervals to listen to the tremulous silence which held everywhere, tense and expectant. Part of him wanted to stretch out his arms to the boy and claim him but he knew he must do nothing on his own direction, only wait and listen. He had been patient for a long time and he could not risk interfering with what would surely come to pass. He climbed the stairs slowly, occasionally pausing to look down into the gloomy well of the hall. The scream told him there was a battle raging for the soul of the boy, that the powers of darkness were mustering their forces. They would not lightly relinquish their hold on the boy, because they knew too well the importance of the part he would play in bringing healing. He knew, too, that the same powers still sought to sow doubt in his own conviction, confuse the clarity of his vision with broken and distorted images. Sometimes he heard whispers in his head, urging, beguiling, pretending to be the true voice, trying to deceive him, but he knew them to be false messengers, borne to him on wings of evil.

Time was short. He thought of the names listed in the books – the great catalogue of the smitten, the host consumed by the creeping sickness spreading out and infecting more and more. Every day, more names to be added, filling the crowded pages. Every day, more tumbling into the pit. Affliction settling like a plague and brooding on the land, infecting the souls of men and women. Soon, with God's grace, he would no longer have to record and preserve the names of the dead, soon it would no longer be necessary.

At the top of the stairs he looked towards the half-opened doorway of his son's room, hesitated, then pushed it fully open. Orange street light seeped into the room and beyond that stretched the glittering frieze of the city below. He did not go in but absorbed it all – the garish posters on the wall, clothes and possessions strewn across furniture and floor, drawers open with parts of clothing trailing out. A world of time away, he had hoped that his son would be the one who would grow in grace and be given to him as his helper, but now he knew it could never be. His own son had been smitten by the sickness and was slowly sinking in sin. Could the healing come in time to save him? If only he could look up in faith then it was surely possible. But deep inside himself he felt that his son was already lost. The pain of that knowledge was his burden, the festering wound he must endure unto the end of his days.

Yet he had always loved the boy, loved him even when he had chastised him. He had done everything possible to secure the boy's salvation, but always it had gone wrong, some tare in the wheat, some blight rotting his soul. Even when he had loved him most the boy had turned his back, gone his own way and spurned his guidance. He knew his son hated him but did not know why. Sometimes it was almost as if the sins he committed were intended to hurt him, to punish him for something he did not understand. It had grown worse after the death of the boy's mother, as if the last few years of her life had suppressed parts of him, and when she died some anger or bitterness had burst open and spread the poisonous spores through his being.

He turned back to the landing and suddenly his thoughts turned to the wife who no longer shared his life. Her face formed in the shifting gloom – not the shrinking, tightening face of a pain-wracked body, her dark-ringed eyes deep pools of pain but that of a young woman, alive with laughter. Her face formed so clearly that he stretched out his hand to touch her hair, her dark rich tresses, but as he did so, shadows ebbed into his memory and he felt only the dry, brittle coils of grey which lay lifeless on the hospital pillow like ash. He drew back his hand and stumbled to the top of the stairs. They swam before his eyes. The coils of ash tightened about him, the memory choking him. He swayed gently, rocked by other moments from the confusion of the past. He stretched out his arms towards her and as his feet moved to the edge of the top stair he called out to her, but suddenly the echo of the boy's scream silenced his own voice and the boy's face replaced all others. As if waking from a dream, he pulled back and his hands gripped the wooden banisters. Sitting down, he hugged them like a child, stroking their worn smoothness over and over.

He knew he would not sleep now and he moved down the darkened stairs slowly and carefully, still holding onto the banisters with both hands. At the bottom he switched on the hall light, his eyes blinking wildly with the sudden shock. He opened the cloakroom door and searched through the musty garments until he found his overcoat. It felt heavy but he knew it would be cold outside and then, without locking the door, he slipped into the night, pulling the black coat tightly about him. As he closed the front gate he looked up at what he knew was the boy's room. The curtains were closed but the light was on. He stood looking up at it for some time but in his heart he knew the boy was safe, watched over by his own angels. He would come to no harm. Then he turned away and started to walk. He often walked late at night, a dark solitary figure, unnoticed by the world, following wandering, random paths through those parts of the city which were familiar to him.

He walked for a long time, keeping to the main roads, watching everything, recording carefully all he saw, pausing from time to time to get his breath back. The neon world trembled like a cold night star. He watched it from a distance, frightened that if he went too close it might suck him into its vortex, consume him in its fiery furnace. All about him men and women hurtled headlong towards destruction – young people intent on only the moment's fleeting pleasure. He peered into fast-food shops, the yellow tunnels of video shops, staring at the people inside like a deaf man watching people dancing to some mysterious tune. As he moved from place to place he felt as if he was invisible to the teeming mass of self-absorbed humanity. He hugged the dark lane-ways of shadow, stopped in unlit doorways and turned his face away from the lights of passing cars. Soon, though, he would make himself known. Make himself known, not as a scourge but as a servant and instrument of light. Flashing signs dazzled his eyes. A drunk staggered towards him then lurched away again, oblivious to his presence. Two girls skipped by, engrossed in their own conversation. A dog sniffed at his heels, then vanished.

He turned off the main road into the web of narrow streets, where television sets transformed the narrow ornament-lined windows into grey grottoes of light. Sometimes he registered broken voices, snatches of conversations, fragments of curtained lives. Past breeze-blocked houses waiting for demolition and open walls where tattered remnants of wallpaper fluttered forlornly like failed dreams. Past painted walls where sprayed writing choked the bricks, like overgrown vines competing for space. On a stretch of waste-ground a bonfire climbed into the night sky, a heaped tumble of meshed rubbish knitted together by the discarded fabric of the world. A flag jutted out of its apex, and somewhere inside its base glowed the red tips of lighted cigarettes where its custodians sat entombed in all-night vigil. He felt a burst of sadness in him. So many lost, so many smitten, untouched and unhealed, stumbling blindly to their fate. Then it was replaced by a deep spring of love for the suffering seed of humanity which huddled all around him in these crumbling streets. He longed to shout out, to gather them close to him, shelter them from the storm. Soon it would be time. His eyes explored the star-studded sky which arched over him and awed him into worship, and his walk took on a trance-like quality as he wandered, indifferent to the direction he was following.

Eventually, tiredness brought him back to a consciousness of where he was. He turned back and followed the embankment, then sat down and watched the shimmer of light glitter the blackness of the water. He rested himself, aware for the first time of how far he had walked and of the growing coldness of the night air. As he pulled the collar of his coat up around his neck a police landrover drove slowly past, decreasing its speed to look at him, then continued on its way. His head dropped onto his chest and his eyes closed in a fitful drowse. Strange images danced before him – three great white swans bursting from the darkness of the water with flapping wings dripping silver beads of light; all the bonfires of the city merged together in one giant, burning bush which burned but was never consumed; the still, small voice of God speaking to him from the heart of the flames; a spectral figure walking on the water then sinking into its blackness.

Suddenly, a hand touched his shoulder. He jerked upwards with a start.

'You all right, Mister?'

He turned to see a young man standing behind him, dressed in a sweatshirt and jeans. He nodded his head in reply and rubbed a hand across his eyes, trying to focus with greater clarity.

'Here, take a drop of this – it'll keep the cold from biting,' the youth said, holding out a wine bottle towards him.

Standing up, he shook his head in refusal, then placed his hand on the young man's shoulder and looked into his face. He wanted to say something from his heart, but the words slipped away like fish out of a net. The youth stared at him with puzzled eyes, then stepped back a little.

'You all right, Pops? You're not thinking of going for a midnight swim – you'd sink like a stone in that coat.'

He took a slug of wine and offered the bottle again, wiping its top with the palm of his hand.

'Whosoever drinketh of this shall thirst again, but whosoever drinketh of the water that I shall give him shall never thirst.'

He spoke the words gently, then turned away on his homeward journey. As he walked away, he heard the young man shouting something after him, but already his mind was fastened on other things and the words were lost. His step took on an urgency. It was the early hours of a new day and the roads were almost deserted, apart from a few taxis shuttling across the city on their final journeys. A man cycled past him on an unlit bicycle, a satchel slung over his shoulder. From some undefined spot he heard a man and woman curse each other in high, bitter voices, then as they faded a gradual calm seeped into the night, quietening the pulse that had raced so fiercely throughout the day. Streets slipped into sleep and a brooding stillness settled on the world. He continued on his way, stopping from time to time to rest, a dark veiled figure unperceived by the world.

A long time later, he began the final climb to his home, his breathing heavy and his steps laboured. He was almost there, his house finally in sight, when suddenly he pulled himself into the pool of shadows from an overhanging tree. A car was stopped outside his house, and in the light from the open door he could see his son get out, then pause to talk to the two men in the front seats. He was close enough to see their faces. His chest grew tight and he could hear the loudness of his breathing. He felt unsteady on his feet and leant against the hedge for support. He looked at his son again but this time he saw him in his memory – standing with him at the bedside as they looked down on the shrunken face, the cheekbones pushing through the drawn skin, dull braids of grey coiled coldly like serpents on the pillow. He closed his eyes, held onto the hedge for support, as the slamming of the car door brought him back to the present moment. He turned his face away as the car sped past him. He waited for a few moments before slipping into the house. It was as silent as he had left it. He climbed the stairs slowly, knowing without looking that the square of yellow light filtering into the garden came from the garage.

BEFORE, THEY HAD spoken to him in many different ways: the flight of a solitary bird, the pattern on a decaying leaf, the settling of dust on a window ledge. Above all, they had woven their threaded whispers through the silence which settled like snow on the farm house, and at night, when dreams beat wildly about his head like dark-winged bats, they screamed their fervent fury. Now they sought new ways to speak to him. An invisible finger scrawled messages of hate on gable walls, black spider lettering scuttling across pitted brick and flaking cement. As he sat beside his mother in the taxi on the way to the hospital, he read their message on each wall they passed, flicking through the street corners like the pages of a book. Black silhouettes were emblazoned on painted blue skies and the invisible finger moved slowly and deliberately, scoring the words deep into his mind. Sometimes they fingered his face until he felt as if he was walking down a long tunnel where webbed filament clung to his skin.

His mother sat tense and alert, her eyes flitting fretfully

over territory she knew was hostile, but her ears did not hear the voices. She sat as if she had a bad taste in her mouth and when the taxi stopped outside the hospital she seemed to have a momentary hesitation, almost as if she was considering telling the driver to take them home again. But she paid the fare, carefully handing over the correct amount, and then placed her purse deep in her handbag.

He didn't want to get out of the back of the taxi, but she encouraged him with a nod of her head and a tight smile which barely hid her fear. They huddled together on the pavement, exposed and vulnerable, before they followed other visitors into the hospital. Plastic doors flapped open and a reassuringly recognizable smell flowed over them. Feet echoed in the tiled corridors as porters pushed wagons of laundry. His mother looked again at the appointment card and consulted a uniformed security man for directions. His radio crackled with static as he re-directed them to a different building. They retraced their steps and walked tentatively through the sprawling grounds where parked cars filled every possible space and ambulances moved in and out. He furtively studied each passing face and walked close to his mother, their syn-chronized steps giving the appearance of a purpose they did not feel.

A man wearing a blue dressing gown over his pyjamas strolled by, indifferent to their stares. Pigeons stuttered across their path, their green heads washed by the sunlight. A police landrover sat with its engine running and the back door open no more than a few inches. Then a nurse directed them to their destination and in a few minutes a receptionist pointed them to a waiting area. His mother sniffed dismissively as she inspected the green plastic chairs with their stains and cracks, the mess of magazines spilled across a wooden table, and the plastic coffee cups which sat uncollected underneath it. He stared at the posters on the wall and listened to the receptionist typing in her glass-fronted office. Two doctors in white coats appeared then walked off down a corridor. The typing continued while his mother's eyes inspected more of the surroundings, holding her bag tightly in her lap as if someone was likely to steal it.

A woman approached them wearing a blue suit and white blouse, and in her hand she carried a large brown envelope. It was the doctor they had been sent to see. He looked into her face as she smiled at him. She knew his name and talked as if she knew all about him. They followed her down the long corridor until they came to an open door, where she paused and showed them in with an outstretched arm. She offered him a seat and presented him with a set of comics to read while she took his mother into an inner office. If he sat still and silent, he could hear snatches of their voices through the frosted glass. After a few minutes they came out, smiling in unison at him.

'Well, Samuel, I think it's time for you and I to get to know each other. What do you say?'

He looked at his mother and she nodded her agreement, but he stayed in his seat and held onto the unopened comics.

'Everything's all right, Samuel. Dr Rollins wants to help. She's helped lots of people your age. Go and talk to her,' his mother said.

Still holding onto the comics he rose and followed the doctor into the inner office. As she closed the door, he glimpsed his mother standing, clutching her bag.

There were plants in the room and coloured posters of animals. The doctor sat down on a chair which was angled towards his, close enough for him to smell her scent, and when he glanced up at her from time to time, he could see a light shadow of perspiration on her upper lip.

'How do you like living in the city, Samuel?'

His hands rolled up the comics tightly.

'I suppose it's a big change from living on a farm. I'm sure it'll take a while to get used to it.'

He pulled his feet back under the chair. Behind her squatted a green metal filing cabinet, watching and listening.

'I've often thought it must be really interesting to live on a farm. Hard work I'm sure, too, of course.'

She paused and smiled at him. Little beads of perspiration had formed on her upper lip. A breeze from the partly-opened window rustled some leaves on a plant sitting on the window ledge. A mobile of metal birds hanging from the ceiling turned slowly.

'Your mother tells me that you don't talk very much any more, Samuel. Your mother tells me too that you've been having bad dreams.'

Framed certificates on the wall stared down at him, their seals dark pupils encased in glass. His hands clutched the sides of the chair until his knuckles whitened.

'Would you tell me about your dreams?'

The birds turned more quickly, their metal wings

glinting coldly in the light. He felt her trying to take him where he could not go. He started to run down the long tunnel of himself, pulling each door tightly closed behind him, and although thick strands of web tried to fasten to him as he ran, he brushed them aside with frantic hands.

'It's all right, Samuel. If you don't want to tell me, it's okay.'

He glanced quickly back at her to see how close she had come in her pursuit. Her green eyes smiled at him like a set trap.

'Sometimes using words is very hard and very painful. I understand that, so right now if you don't want to speak, it's all right.'

She stood up and went to a shelf behind her desk. Her black hair was fastened with a bronze-coloured clasp. She took down a sheet of white paper and a tub of felt-tipped pens, then cleared a space on her desk and laid the paper down.

'I know it might sound childish, but what I'd like you to do is draw something for me. I'd like you to draw one of your dreams. You can draw it any way you want and use any of the colours. I'm going to leave you here so you can give it a go without me looking over your shoulder. Bring your chair right up to the desk while I have a chat with your mum. Don't be frightened. Trust me.'

She opened the door and went out.

The white page stretched in front of him like a sheet of ice. His fingers cautiously touched its coldness then pulled away. The pens bristled like arrows in a quiver. Above his head the sharp-beaked birds hovered menacingly. He looked at the page again. It gently called him on, inviting him to skate across its surface, and he could hear her voice in his head urging him to trust her. He imagined her standing on the other side of the desk with her arms outstretched, enticing him forward. Step onto the ice. Just a little step and she would reach out and catch him if there was any danger. He took the top off a pen. Trust her. Step out across the ice. Just one little step – that was all it would take.

Suddenly the wail of a passing siren filled the room and his whole body was shaken by doubt. It was a trap. He would step out and the ice would crack beneath him, plunging him into the dark waters below. He would plummet into its black heart and then the ice would close over again above his head, trapping him in its frozen depths.

He took the black marker and scored it feverishly across the page, obliterating as much of the blinding whiteness as he could. He did it until his wrist was sore and the smell of the ink soaked his senses, and as he did so, the glass eyes smiled down at him and the birds rotated gently once more. Outside, he could hear the doctor talking to his mother.

'. . . suffering from post-trauma stress disorder. A bit of a mouthful, I know, but not uncommon, I'm afraid. We can help him, but it will take time and careful therapy.'

He put the cap back on the pen. Inside the filing cabinet, something creaked. The leaves of a plant fluttered then fell still again. The tone of his mother's voice was changing. She sounded weary and suddenly full of doubt.

'I know you mean well, Doctor, and I know you can

heal many sicknesses nowadays, but only God's peace can heal my son now.'

He rose from the chair, pushed it under the desk and went out to his mother. He stood beside her and she placed a hand on his shoulder. They both wanted to go and he closed his ears to the doctor's voice which followed them out of the office and down the long corridor with its polished floor, and doors with names on them.

A week later, on a Sunday night, his mother took him to God. It wasn't the new church they had started to attend, but a large tent on playing fields close to where the river curved its ponderous course. They walked along the embankment where young men jogged past breathlessly, and young couples strolled hand in hand, to where the tent squatted large and white.

Two men standing at the entrance gave them hymn sheets as they entered and a third guided them to seats. On a tiered level, a choir sat grouped around a pulpit. They were much younger than the choirs he was used to, and when they sang they clapped their hands and swayed gently from side to side. People in the congregation clapped along with them and there was a feeling of expectancy which he did not associate with church. He looked up at the roof of the tent where ropes and poles connected like the spokes of an umbrella. His mother bowed her head in prayer, her lips moving silently, synchronized with her soul. He wondered if small birds ever found themselves trapped inside the dome of the tent.

Then the clapping grew louder and the singing became more insistent. A couple of rows in front of where they were seated, two girls stood up and raised their arms in the

DAVID PARK

air as if they were surrendering to something. Their heads dropped back onto their shoulders and their faces searched upwards. More and more people filed their way into the tent until all the seats were taken, while some people stood in clusters at the back.

The evangelist appeared from somewhere behind the choir, gripped both sides of the lectern and bowed his head solemnly, and when he looked up, his face was smiling down at them as if he knew each one of them personally and was pleased they had come.

As he spoke, the music continued to play softly in the background and his voice was a strange mixture of a local accent and something partly American. When he lifted both his hands into the air, the tent fell silent, all the rustling and coughing fading away, until the only sound was far-off traffic.

'Let us go to the Lord in prayer. Our heavenly Father, as we come before You tonight, as we approach the mercy seat in prayer, we look to You for Your blessing. Look down on this assembly tonight and bless us with Thy presence. Shut out all things that would distract or hinder us from hearing Thy voice and send Thy Holy Spirit to guide our worship. We know that here tonight there are those with heavy hearts weighed down by their burden of sin, and those who are afflicted in body and soul. Be graciously near to them and help them this very night to make that journey of faith that they might know the power of Thy salvation. Thou who calmed the storm, quieten now our souls and help us to hear only Thy voice. In Thy holy name we ask it.'

A chorus of affirmation burst out around the tent.

They sang one of the hymns from the sheet they had
been given, and some voices in the choir sang high
parts, weaving in and out of the melody. Many people
raised their hands and some linked with others in a raised
chain. The whole service was different to what he was
accustomed to, unpredictable in both pattern and style,
and when the preacher read from the Bible, his voice too
had an unfamiliar cadence. The passage he read was about
the woman who had an illness described as an 'issue of
blood' who was cured when she touched the hem of
Christ's garment. Amidst all the heaving mass of people,
Christ had known that someone had touched Him. The
preacher's relentless voice filled the tent, rolling round it
and billowing out the sides, and the words soared across
his heart like swallows, diving and darting into the dark
spaces. Sometimes, too, it felt as though the preacher's
eyes rested on him, and he could see deep inside him.

He was comparing life to a journey, and beside him
his mother sat with the white handkerchief wreathing her
hand. She seemed to be carried along by the words.

'Besides being a strange journey, it's also a swift one.
The moment we believe, we receive life. Between God
and man exists a great chasm, a deep turbulence of sin.
Oh, sinner, is your soul tossed on that sea tonight? Are
you weary and troubled in spirit? There have been many
attempts to bridge this chasm, and indeed, all around us we
hear the voices of those who preach reformation, revolu-
tion, and so on – poor, misguided people who think this or
that external change can alter the condition of man's heart.
Well, I say to those people tonight – read the word of God,
search the scriptures, for you know, dear friends, all our

righteousness is as filthy rags. That's right, all our own efforts at change are worthless, pitiful gestures doomed to failure. Yes, and yet this journey is such a swift one that it only requires faith. It's true that it may take a man a good deal of time to approach the door, but it's also true that it only takes a moment to enter. A single moment, the twinkling of an eye – that's all it takes to enter into a living union with God. Oh poor, travel-weary sinner, it's a swift journey and now is the appointed time, and now is the moment of salvation.'

From close by came the sound of someone sobbing. In the choir, men sat with their heads in their hands. There was no escape from the voice. It pursued him no matter where he tried to run.

'Know, too, that this journey is a simple one. Through Christ's atoning death, God has dealt with sin and the simplicity of the journey makes it possible for everyone to partake. All you have to do is believe. Everyone can come – the poor and the rich, the learned and the ignorant, the young and the old. Praise God, there's no discrimination in heaven! But sometimes, I confess, friends, that I feel the very simplicity of God's free gift is beyond the comprehension of our perverse and wayward generation. Oh yes, if salvation was a matter of works, then I believe some people would feel happier. Can they not understand that the price has been paid in full? And how, indeed, shall we escape if we ignore such an offer of salvation? This journey is one that will satisfy your soul. There are many here tonight who could stand on this very spot and testify to that. It's a good and rich life, free from the taint of sin, free from condemnation, and it's yours,

yours for the asking. Oh, friend, could I put it any more simply? Come, taste the richness of God's mercy. Come, bring your heavy burdens and lay them down at the foot of the cross.

'Think now of that woman we read about who touched Christ's garment. What made her touch different from all the rest was that she touched in faith. And the moment she did that, she was made well. That same power to cure is waiting here for you tonight. Whether it's from a terrible burden of sin, or some bodily affliction, it's here for all to experience. Don't put off this decision a moment longer. Sinner, hear the voice speaking to your heart. Don't delay, come in faith and ask for forgiveness. Whether you're in the autumn of your life, or even if you're in the seed time, now is the appointed time.'

He felt like a little bird trapped in the great dome of the tent, desperate to break into the safety of the sky. The words were the bars against which his wings beat frantically until they were bruised and broken.

'Take this step tonight; move from death into life. Forget the people sitting next to you. Forget everything that would hinder and hold you back. Come and touch the hem of the garment. Come to Jesus. Come!'

HE RANG THE bell. He had been right to wait until he heard the voice, right to resist the temptation to rush too quickly towards this moment. Everything had its appointed time and it was for him only to be ready for it. He had not rehearsed what he would say but would speak the words that were given to him. The bell had the same tone as his own, the door the same colour of leaded glass. He looked through a square into the blue world beyond. The door at the end of the hall was open and he could see into the kitchen. As the bell's sound faded away he stared through a red square and wondered if he should ring it again, but as he raised his hand he saw her coming down the hall, a hand smoothing back her hair. He stepped back off the doorstep and waited.

'Mrs Anderson? My name is Henry Ellison. I live next door. I've come to welcome you and your son to the avenue.'

He stood, searching her eyes. She smiled at him.

'That's very kind of you, Mr – Mr Ellison. Thank

70

you very much.'

He stood on, smiling back at her.

'We've just about got ourselves organized. We seemed to be living out of tea chests for a while, but it's more or less sorted out now.'

He looked past her down the length of the hall. The boy was peering at him round the living-room door, a pale moon of a face, watching him with sharp, curious eyes. Their eyes met for a second and then the boy vanished into the living-room. He felt a wave of exultation break over him.

'Well, thank you, Mr Ellison, for calling. It was very kind of you.'

He stood motionless, staring at where the boy had been.

'Are you all right, Mr Ellison?'

A breeze moved the hall light.

'Mr Ellison?'

He looked back at her. She was watching him with a puzzled expression. Her hand was on the door handle – she would close it soon.

'I'd just like to offer, Mrs Anderson, my deepest sympathy for your loss and to say that if there's anything I can do to be of help, you only have to ask. I'm never far from the house and you only have to ask.'

She thanked him again and he could see that she was gently starting to close the door.

'I was wondering, Mrs Anderson, if you'd let me tidy up your garden – you know, take it in hand for you. The house has been empty for so long that it's got into a bit of a state. I'm retired now, so I've plenty of time on my hands and I'd be more than glad to do it for you.'

She hesitated, but her hand had dropped from the door.

'It's very kind of you to offer and your own garden certainly looks very well. I was just admiring it the other day. But it's a big job, bigger than I realized and I was thinking of getting someone in. It's very thoughtful of you to offer, but I couldn't impose on you like that.'

'You wouldn't be imposing at all,' he insisted. 'It'd be a pleasure. I like the garden, and I've the time to do it. I always feel closest to God's handiwork in a garden.'

'Are you sure?' she asked.

'I'm sure. It'd be no trouble at all. I'll start first thing in the morning.'

'Only if you're sure you wouldn't be taking on too much.'

He shook his head, turned to go, then paused and looked once more into her eyes.

'Maybe the boy would like to help me,' he said softly.

'Samuel? Yes, maybe he would. I'll ask him. We'll see you, then, tomorrow, Mr Ellison, and thank you for calling.'

He closed the gate carefully, looking back at the col-oured glass in the door, then glanced up at the bedroom to see the boy's face vanish behind a curtain, like the moon behind clouds.

In the morning, he put on his working clothes and boots, and went to the garage to gather his working tools. He opened the curtains, sat down on the wooden chair and laced the boots, tying the laces tightly and tucking the bottom of his trousers into his socks. His eyes flitted round the scattered contents, never resting anywhere for more than a second, then gradually, almost against his will, they returned to the same heaped monument of rubbish. Nothing appeared to have changed, nothing appeared to have moved. He felt frightened to look too closely or go any nearer to it, frightened even to look at it for more than a moment. A spider scuttled across the floor and a rafter above his head gave a sudden creak as if stretched too tightly. He looked down at his boots. One of the knots was loose and he opened it and re-tied it, stood up and stamped his feet on the ground, sending little clouds of dust into the air, then lifted a spade and a hoe down from hooks, carried them outside and propped them against the garage wall. After cleaning the lawnmower with a wire brush he took it outside also. Then he reached over the hedge and set the tools down in the neighbouring garden. He lifted the lawnmower through one of the gaps in the hedge, its weight making him stumble a little.

As he stood looking up at the house, the woman came out of the back doorway, drying her hands on a towel. She smiled at him almost as if she was surprised that he had really come. He had to reassure her again that he was happy to do the work for her, but as he spoke his eyes searched the house for some sign of the boy. He could sense him close by, almost hear the beat of his heart, but he could find no trace of that pale face. The woman was talking to him, telling him things about the boy, but they faded out of his consciousness as his eyes flicked from window to window and back to the open door.

'I understand,' he said. 'Don't worry about anything. I understand about Samuel. I understand about the boy.'

She kept on drying her hands with the towel, turning them again and again inside its folds.

'You said you're retired now, Mr Ellison.'

'Yes, five years now. I used to be with the Council – Parks and Cemeteries. I suppose working in the garden is a way of keeping my hand in. Makes me feel useful, keeps me busy.'

'It's very good of you to take on this jungle. I've spoken to Samuel and I think he'd like to help, but I let him do things in his own time. I see you're keen to start, so I'll let you get on with it. I'll put the kettle on in a little while and give you a shout.'

She turned and walked back to the house, carrying the towel in her hand like a cardigan. The house looked down at him, giving no clue as to the boy's whereabouts. He started to cut the grass, struggling a little because of the length of the grass and frequently having to empty the grass box. He dumped the cut grass on the other side of the fence at the bottom of the garden. Although he could not see the boy, he knew he was watching him. He worked steadily trying to keep his mind on the work in hand, but so many thoughts rolled round his head that he worked mechanically, no longer fully aware of what he was doing. Sometimes he forgot to empty the box and bits of grass spewed out of its sides and left a snail-trail behind him.

It grew warmer and he rolled up the sleeves of his shirt, then once more carried the full box to the back fence and dropped it onto the growing pile. When he turned round the boy was standing beside the mower. His heart felt as though a hand had gripped it, but he smiled and forced himself to walk slowly towards the boy. When he reached him, he dropped the box to the ground and rested his hand lightly on the boy's shoulder.

'You've come. I knew you would. It's been a long wait, but you've finally come to help me.'

His heart melted into a stream of thanks and he felt a course of expectancy run through him. The boy held a handful of cut grass in his hand and it filtered slowly through his opening fingers. He wanted to gather the boy to him, but all he did was gently pat his shoulder.

'The Lord has sent you to me, Samuel, to be my helper. There's so much work to be done but together we can see it through.'

The boy dropped the remainder of the grass, then moved away to where the rake leaned against the hedge and began to gather up the trail of grass cuttings. He smiled as he watched the boy. He was a good worker, this child who had been lent unto the Lord. Together they would achieve great things. With a feeling of lightness he went back to his own work and now each time the grass box was filled the boy would carry it for him and empty it behind the fence. They worked silently together, the steady rhythm keeping them close, and soon the last of the grass was cut. As they finished, the kitchen door opened and the boy's mother called them to come in for a cup of tea. He knocked his boots against the wall of the house, then scraped them on the rubber mat. The boy had already entered and was sitting on a stool, sipping a glass of orange juice.

'There you are,' she said, as she poured his tea then handed him a plate with biscuits and some home-baked buns. 'You made short work of that lawn – I hope it didn't take too much out of you. I hope this boy did his share.'

'Samuel worked hard. He's a good worker. But we've still got the hedges to clip and then we'll have to think about doing something with the borders.'

'That's a lot of work you're taking on. Take your time – there's no rush to get it done. I'm just very grateful. I don't think we could have managed it on our own.'

The boy watched him over the rim of his glass.

'It doesn't take much for a garden to get out of control, but when it does it's not easy to put right. Nothing grows faster than weeds. You just turn your back for a couple of minutes and there's an army of weeds choking the life out of everything. A garden's something you have to keep on top of all the time.'

He sipped his tea and watched the boy drain his glass. He looked younger than his twelve years. It suddenly struck him how strange it was that God had chosen an old man such as himself, and a young boy to be the servants of His will. Yet, did it not say that God had chosen the weak and lowly things of this world to confound the mighty, and when God spoke to man, did He not spurn the flames and the great wind, choosing to speak in a still, small voice? That same still, small voice would soon speak to all men's hearts, breathe life into the dead clay of their souls. Soon.

'I suppose we'll have to wait until the autumn, Mr Ellison, before we plant anything.'

'Aye, that's right, but when we get some of the borders cleaned up, we'll transfer some bedding plants from my place. It's a bit late in the day but it'll give you a bit of colour for the rest of the summer.'

'You'll have to let me pay you something for your trouble.'

'I couldn't accept any money, Mrs Anderson. Seeing plants take and grow is payment enough and it's in a garden full of flowers that God reveals a little of His being, for Solomon in all his glory wasn't arrayed in such beauty as the lilies of the field.'

'You know your Bible, Mr Ellison.'

He nodded his head and looked at the boy holding his empty glass tightly as if it were a chalice.

'And you took the boy's name from the Bible. "She called his name Samuel, saying Because I have asked him of the Lord." Asked of the Lord and then lent unto Him to do His work.'

'Samuel was the first name me and his father agreed on. We didn't even bother with a middle name,' she said, ruffling the boy's hair. 'Do you have any children, Mr Ellison?'

'I have a son.'

He took a final sip from his tea, then stood up.

'I'd better be getting back to it. Thank you for the tea.'

As he walked down the garden he could feel the boy following him. A son. He almost felt now that this boy was his son. In many ways he was closer, more real than his own. The boy was a sacred trust, a gift that he would let no one take away from him or harm. Apart they were weak – straws scattered in the wind – but together they would be strong enough to carry out what had been ordained. The boy spoke to him all the time, strengthening his resolve, driving away the sinful doubts which lingered in the back of his mind, and helping him to understand the great mystery more clearly. The boy's presence made him feel complete, carried him closer to that moment when healing would pour down upon a people riven by sickness, like water gushing from a rock. In that moment, all the dark corners of himself would be transfigured by God's light and all the secret, barren parts of his life would turn green and bud with new life. His soul sang with the memory of miracles – water into wine, withered arms healed, sight to the blind – until they flowed and blurred into one joyous dance of the miraculous. And in his heart burnt a bright flame of love, love for the sick and the lost, those dying without faith or hope. He counted the hours and days until God would finally reveal His plan and the healing would begin.

The boy looked over at him and told him to be still and patient, to wait calmly for that moment. He nodded his understanding, then continued hoeing the bed which ran along the hedge, stooping from time to time to pick out the weeds he had uprooted. The boy crouched close by and pulled out grass and weeds with his hands, tearing at them as if his life depended upon it.

HIS MOTHER WAS very excited, taking pleasure in her preparations and checking the picnic for things she knew had already been included. She talked continuously, fussing about and looking through the kitchen window to check the weather. The trip was supposed to be for him, but he knew she was pursuing some memory of the past, a memory which warmed and consoled her, and he knew she wanted him to be touched by its gentle healing. The idea had been planted in her mind by his uncle, but she had chosen to keep the trip for the two of them, as if afraid that sharing it might dilute its power. It meant nothing to him but he did not want to spoil it for her.

They were to catch the ten o'clock train to Portrush and everything they needed was packed into two shopping bags. There were rows of sandwiches in plastic containers, a flask of tea, a rug and waterproofs, and more things than they would need. As they set off down the hill towards the bus stop a haze hung over the city. They carried a bag each and walked in step while his mother talked a great deal,

79

describing all the attractions of the seaside resort. It was a Saturday morning and a bus came quickly to carry them into town. When they got off just before the bridge he looked at his mother with some confusion. No one else had got off with them and there was nothing to point the way to a station, but his mother led the way across the road and stepped out with a confidence that reassured him. But the confidence did not last long as they turned down the quayside and suddenly came to a halt. He looked up at his mother's face. She was glancing about her nervously as she set her bag down and plucked at her hair with the freed hand.

'The station isn't here. It used to be just there.'

They stared in silence at the missing station. She clock-worked about him, refusing to believe her own eyes. He looked at the stains on the pavement and its moss-filled cracks. His hand was sore from carrying the bag and a thin white welt had formed across his fingers. A man in a bright yellow jacket appeared, brushing the street, and when his mother asked him where the station was, he smiled at her and gave them directions. Even if the station had still been there, it would not have been the right one. She made a little joke to hide her embarrassment and when the man had moved away, she picked up her bag and hurried them on to their new destination.

They arrived with only five minutes to spare, but there were others later than them – a group of skinheads in T-shirts and jeans, bristling with tattoos and noise. Each of them carried two six-packs of beer and they shouted and whooped along the length of the platform. His mother turned her back with disdain and ushered him onto the train. It was a connecting train with a central aisle and tables set between groups of four seats. They sat opposite each other in the window seats and his mother spread their possessions over the other two seats, as if making a territorial claim for invisible travelling companions. She rummaged in the bag and handed him a little carton of orange juice and he speared the tiny silver hole with the straw, then sat back and watched as the train began to move.

The start of all journeys filled him with misgivings. It always felt good to be moving from where he was, to be putting space between himself and his pursuers, but it also brought a fear of being stopped at the last minute, caught at the point of attempted escape. He knew they would resist such attempts to outstretch their reach, knew they would seek to watch him closely in case he might try to break free. He scanned the world outside while he held the carton of juice close to his face. The train crawled past the backs of terraced houses where the scabbed brickwork festered in sores of black and brown, while rotting wooden window frames, often painted in ugly, bright colours, framed small windows. Windows bordered by thin strips of curtain. Windows watching. A sudden glimpse of a faceless head pushed him back into his seat. The train gathered speed, his mind urging it on, the fingers of his left hand pressing into the fabric of the seat, as if pushing an accelerator. Past rows of blackened roofs with missing slates replaced by lighter-coloured ones; television aerials jutting at crazy angles from chimneys; pigeon lofts – makeshift patchworks of felt-covered scraps of wood, balancing on precarious structures. At intervals, derelict houses, their roofs punctured like colanders, with pigeons fluttering in and out of the holes. Fragile purple weeds growing in cracks and crevices, and by the side of the track, foxgloves leaning forwards out of steep banks.

He glimpsed another bonfire – a piled tangle of debris squatting on waste-ground, a windblown haystack of the unwanted and discarded. Past gable walls where rungs of bunting made bright ladders of the streets. And everywhere there was a wall, or square of concrete, the spider writing spread its messages of warning and hate. The words spat at him, hissing white-teethed whispers into his head and as he shivered and turned his head away, the train assumed a quicker and more repetitive rhythm. Across the aisle sat an elderly man reading a newspaper. The woman opposite him seemed to be his wife.

His mother took the empty carton out of his hand and placed it in a polythene bag she had brought for rubbish. He felt reluctant to let it go. The bright orange of the carton glowed through the thin skin of polythene. A little dribble of orange had dripped onto the table and vibrated gently like mercury, until his mother took a tissue and wiped the whole table, her hand rubbing furiously at invisible stains like a windscreen wiper out of control. The elderly man looked at her for a few seconds from behind his paper, then flicked his eyes back to the pages.

The city eventually gave way to fields and the countryside, hedgerows acting as gradations of speed and distance. Ploughed fields, cattle grazing, indifferent to their passing; lonely little farms sheltering in hollows; others perched boldly on skylines, braving the winds which tattered the dye-daubed sheep, and bent the gaunt trees into contorted and bitter shapes. A familiar landscape echoing in his memory. He looked away again, tried to silence the echoes, let his heart beat in syncopated rhythm with the motion of the train, rocked himself gently, let his being run with the rocking, rolling momentum of the train, carrying him away from the past, taking him to some new place. Past empty stations and houses, roads and rivers, momentary glimpses, fragments of the past jolting his memory.

As more days and weeks went by, he found himself beginning to think of it. Not all of it, but just the small parts he could control, the parts he could rearrange into new shapes. At the start his whole being had sought to deny his memory, refusing to accept his own experience, but now he crept lightly towards it, ready at any moment to flee its grasp, ready to block it out once more with disbelief. As the train hurtled forward, he felt increasingly detached from time and place, in a safer nowhere world where he was moving from place to place so quickly that perhaps he could not be caught. Cautiously, he circled the moment, always keeping it at a safe distance. Now he found himself trying to imagine different paths to that moment with different exits and different outcomes.

In his mind he manufactured them with bitter ease – a change in the weather as rain fell in a deluge, making the grass steeped and sodden; something wrong with the tractor's engine – dark spurts of smoke pouring from the innards; his mother calling them back to the house because cattle had broken loose from a field. There was no end to the long list which he constructed, and even though some were as small as the smallest stone they, too, could have changed the most terrible thing that had happened. And as he pondered how so many small things could easily have prevented such a big thing, he wondered once again why God did not care enough to let one of these small things happen. Only a second's intervention, the tiniest drop of caring could have saved his father, and the more he thought about it, the more he thought that God had helped the men kill his father. He had given them the shelter of the hedgerow, the soft light of the setting sun, the silent grass under their feet. He had kept his father's mind concentrated on the work he was doing. Though He could have done so easily, He had given no warning shout, had not swallowed their evil in the burning light of the sun.

Why did God care about his father so little? He could not find a reason even though he searched for a long time. Perhaps his father had done something he did not know about, some terrible thing for which God had chosen to punish him, but he could not think that it was true, and in his head he heard his mother's voice saying, 'He never did harm to anyone.' Over and over, 'He never did harm to anyone,' and the more he thought of those words, the more he began to hate God, to hate Him for not caring enough to do even a little thing to save his father. He hated Him with a little flame of intensity and was glad he had not trusted the minister's words. He felt, too, that God returned his hatred, because if it was not His will, why did He allow such fear to clutch at his heart, and so many dark spirits to pursue him by day and night?

He thought, too, of the old man, the old man who

seemed to know so much about him, but whose words were inexplicable riddles which made no sense. The old man talked about God a great deal, as if he understood what He was thinking. Perhaps he knew why God had allowed his father to be killed. As the train sped on, his mother was talking about days long gone when she had visited Portrush, and she was still excited, but the more she tried to reassure them both about the good time they would have, the more doubts sprang up in his mind. Two of the skinheads appeared in the carriage, swaggering down the aisle and pulling themselves forward by the tops of the seats. One of them winked at him, silently offering him a drink from his can of beer, then they were gone, joking and shouting loudly to each other. His mother and the woman opposite shook their heads at each other in silent condemnation.

When they arrived at Portrush, the group of skinheads was first off, jumping from the train while it was still moving. Their whoops and screams punctured the air and one of them banged the window of the carriage as he ran past, but his mother pretended not to notice and concentrated on gathering up their possessions, making sure that everything was safely packed into the shopping bag.

Much of her confidence had drained away, to be replaced by a kind of grim determination that they should both enjoy themselves. It was as if she wanted to prove through this first excursion that it was possible for them to pull themselves out of the hollow in which they found themselves, and move forward with their lives. He understood what she was trying to do, and although the crowded shops and pavements made him uneasy, he tried his best to help her achieve her goal. But right from the start, everything seemed to conspire to defeat them. The weather itself dampened much of their initial enthusiasm, with overcast skies preventing them from spending any time on the beach, and there was an aggressive edge to the bristling crowds which made them both increasingly nervous. At times, he felt as if the people who flowed all around might suddenly swallow them up, or that he would be separated from his mother and swept further and further away by the ebbing tide of faces. The fear made him hold on to her coat as they drifted aimlessly round stores which sold similar seaside novelties, and rows of fast-food shops. Rubbish littered the pavements and sometimes they almost stumbled over groups of young people sitting on the pavements drinking from bottles of wine.

They had their picnic in a shelter facing the sea, and he knew his mother had almost used up what remained of her will. He felt sad for her and wanted to take her burden and carry it on his own shoulders for a while, but did not know how. As his mother poured tea from the flask and they sat cupping the mugs in both hands, both of them knew they did not belong in this place; both wanted to go home, but there were several hours before a train returned to Belfast. He listened as his mother attempted to revive her flagging spirits, trying as always to soldier on, to put on a brave face, but it seemed that the harder she tried, the more things slipped away from her.

As a fine rain began to fall, they made their way into the amusements, despite his mother's obvious reluctance.

He led her by the hand, determined to salvage something from the day and forcing himself to look people in the face with darting deliberate glances. He tried to walk tall and strong, meeting the noise and spark of the screaming machines with unflinching resolve and making his hand touch the surface of the objects which he passed. They went on a machine called the Cyclone, which hurled them towards the surrounding railings, only stopping at the final moment before hurtling them in new directions. His mother gave little gasps of shock, tucked her head into her chest and held on tightly to the safety bar, but he leaned back against the seat and kept his eyes open all the time. The wind streamed through his hair as he hurtled towards the faces spectating at the barriers, but he met their gaze defiantly and then, as the machine slowed down his mother lifted her head and laughed with relief.

They tried other things, spurring each other on with little spurts of unaccustomed recklessness, teasing each other and trying not to be afraid. Sometimes they put money into machines without really knowing how they worked, and did not care when they lost it. His mother bought him a helium-filled parrot. It was the most out-of-character thing he had ever seen her do, but he held the string tightly in case it slipped out of his fingers. It felt almost like they were riding a little wave so he let it carry him, and when they reached the ghost train he did not resist but dragged his mother into one of the tiny carriages. She grew quiet and placed her arm round him protectively, but in the darkness she could not see him smiling at the fluorescent skeletons and tawdry silhouettes which sprang up at them in pathetic counterfeits of fear.

In about an hour they had exhausted the amusements and decided that they would make their way to the station. As they were leaving the arcade there was the sudden sound of screaming and swearing, and as they emerged into the daylight they saw the group of skinheads huddled round one of its members. His mother tried to usher him past, but he turned to stare at the youth in the centre of the gang who was straightening himself up and shaking off the supporting arms draped over his shoulders. As the youth stood up straight, he held his head back and shook his head from side to side like a dog which had just come out of water, and as he did so, bright gouts of blood splashed his white T-shirt. His mother quickened her pace and hurried him on, and as he twisted his head to look, the parrot slipped out of his fingers and soared into the sky. It streamed upwards, the string wriggling like the tail of a tadpole. His mother smiled wryly at him but did not lessen her pace.

The train journey home was long and tedious and the countryside which streamed past seemed flat and lifeless. His mother was quiet now, resting her head against the side of the seat as the rhythm of the train lulled her. He watched her eyes slowly close as she slipped into sleep. Her fitful doze allowed him to study her face and his gaze traced the blue half-moons under her eyes, the fine grey hairs filtering through the brown. She never wore lipstick or make-up and her whole face looked open and vulnerable. He knew the day had been a disappointment to her. She had tried hard to make it work, to grasp hold of something that couldn't be grasped because it had disappeared into the depths of the past. Like so many of her other memories it would be damaged now, splintered into a thousand pieces like glass and the little box in which she stored them would be open for prying hands to finger and destroy.

As he sat and watched her, he knew now that neither of them could escape so easily, and he knew, too, that happiness was not a place to which you could travel. Empty fields flashed by, bound by broken lines of hedgerow. His mother looked sad and lonely, her sleep separating them from each other, and he felt shut out from her, thrown back onto himself and pushed deeper into the safer world he had sought to build about his being. It was a world in which he was sometimes secure, but at this moment he wanted to slip out from the shadowy silence and step towards her, touch her gently and tell her that everything would be all right. He dipped deep inside himself for words, but they spilled like water through his fingers and seeped away into secret places. He felt ringed and hooped with silence and though he stretched out his hand again and again to grasp them, each time he drew it back empty.

A sudden squall of rain slanted across the window. He forced himself to try once more, searching desperately to find some key which would unlock the door he himself had shut, but it could not be found and the knowledge shocked him. Suddenly, what he had thought of as a safe place had snapped closed about him, trapping him in a world he no longer controlled. Opposite him, his mother stirred a little then settled again. Outside it had grown darker and as the lights in the carriage came on, he saw his reflection watching him, his mouth forming silent words, rain running down the glass like tears.

THE BOY FOLLOWED him through the gap in the broken fence and into the field at the back of the houses. Samuel stayed close to him, stepping in his footsteps, shadowing his path up the slope, stopping when he stopped for breath, mirroring his movements. He felt the comfort of his presence and the strength it lent to his resolve. A rising wind blew against them as they zig-zagged up the slope, but they pressed on, his body sheltering the boy from the wind. Sometimes his feet slipped a little and he placed a hand on the ground to steady himself. The sky was a vague, pale wash, as if the deepest colours had been drained from it and all about them the wind pushed the sharp-edged grass in broken rhythms.

There was a rocky outcrop about half-way up the slope and he headed doggedly for it. He pointed it out wordlessly to the boy and knew he understood. There was so much the boy understood already. They had spent a lot of time together in the past few weeks and had managed to get the garden into some sort of shape, tackling a small section at a time, but it was only a trivial prelude to the task that was in hand. He felt himself flowing towards that moment, carried irresistibly towards his appointed destiny. Part of him shrank from that responsibility in the old consciousness of his own inadequacies, but part of him longed for the healing to begin. Every day brought new victims, new names to be added to a long list. As his mind began to reflect on his weaknesses he heard the boy's voice inside his head saying, 'I will be thy mouth and teach thee what thou shalt say,' and in that instant his fears began to subside. They were almost at the outcrop. He turned and smiled at the boy, nodding his head to show that he had heard and understood.

When they reached it they sat down on the blunted slabs of grey rock which jutted out of the slope, sitting side by side to rest and get their breath back after the climb. They looked down at their own houses and then over the terraced levels of roofs into the city below. The boy plucked at some grass and threw the broken blades down towards it, but the wind swirled them aside like bits of confetti.

'There are important things we have to talk about. Some you know already in your heart. You haven't come to this city by chance – it's part of the plan God has for us both. You are not on your own any more, you have been lent unto the Lord.'

He glanced at the boy but he was still staring down into the city below.

'There is a great sickness down there and every day it consumes more and more – men, women, children – it infects everyone, sweeps them into the pit. It's just like in the Bible all over again, when the children of Israel were wandering in the desert, trapped in their sin and backbiting against God, and the people were bitten by fiery serpents. For twenty years the people down there have been stumbling deeper into sin, lost in their hatreds and their prides, turning their hands against each other, turning their backs on God. But God is not mocked, and now we have the fiery serpents and each day the news brings the names of more people who are bitten. Each day there is fresh blood on the lintels and the people are weary and sick, and looking for a way to heal their souls.'

He paused and moved his hand slowly across the view.

'Look down there, Samuel, see how many churches there are. Everywhere you look. See them? Everywhere. But the sickness goes on despite them because they have been weighed in the balance and found wanting. The sickness spreads everywhere all around them and they cannot stop it. And you know why, Samuel? Because the salt has lost its savour and all those churches down there don't mean anything but savourless salt. Thieves in the temple have defiled His house and now they sit down there like empty shells.'

The boy was looking up at him, his pale curious eyes searching to grasp the truth of his words.

'God has chosen us to be His instrument of healing. God has chosen us, Samuel. It's not for us to understand why or know His reasoning, but only to submit to His will, listen to His voice. We must prepare, hold nothing back of ourselves, be ready to carry His truth to the people down there, floundering in their own darkness. It will be very soon – it must be soon before it's too late. I am an old man and God has given you to me as a helpmate. Once I had hoped it might be my own son, but he too has been bitten, bitten by a serpent of hatred and bitterness and now in his blindness and sin he turns his back on God.'

He lifted his eyes to the vague wash of sky and felt the pain of his words. A solitary bird winged overhead, its dark shape printed on the pale background. The boy fingered a stone, turning it slowly over in his hand, holding it as if it was precious.

'It's just you and me now, who can tell them about the healing. When the children of Israel were bitten by the serpents, God told Moses to raise up a brass serpent on a pole and anyone who looked up at it in faith was healed. You remember it, Samuel – a brass serpent on a pole, and anyone who had the faith to look up at it was healed. Can you see it, Samuel? It's how the healing will come again, only this time it won't be a serpent of brass but if we are ready and listen to His voice, God will reveal what it is we must do. And anyone can be healed. We too can share it. God can take away the fear that clutches at your heart, Samuel, take away the pain of your mother's grief. We, too, can be touched by the healing.'

Now the boy was looking at him intently, his red hair ruffled by the wind. He placed his hand on the boy's shoulder, anxious to confirm that he had understood the magnitude of his words, grasped the full knowledge of what he had imparted, and then suddenly, in a pulse of joy, he knew that everything was well. God had prepared the boy's heart for the truth, and the seed his words had sown would soon bear a great harvest. They sat in silence as all about them the wind rustled in the grass and wisps of thistledown floated by.

After a long time, they stood up and set off across the field, following a narrow mud path which had been worn flat. In a lower field two horses hugged a hedge and sheltered from the wind which disturbed their manes and tails. Suddenly, something stirred in them, and they tossed their heads and careered in a galloping arc, pursuing shifting patterns of light. They stood and watched for a while and his soul felt free and light, as if it had cast off its fetters and was running free with the horses. His happiness made him want to walk for ever, as if going back down to the houses might destroy the joy he felt inside himself. He saw the boy's mother in her garden hanging out washing. He pointed her out to the boy. He knew she would not mind them going for the walk – they had worked hard at the garden.

He showed the boy all the places he knew, pointing out things, naming plants, telling him where there was a rabbit warren. They came down the other side of the slope where workmen were building new houses and they crouched on their haunches watching the men work. A yellow bulldozer was clearing a new site, pushing great scoops of earth to one side. Then a lorry arrived delivering stones and tipping them into a grey mound. Two men used long-handled shovels to push out the remaining stones, their arms working as if they were paddling a canoe. They crouched in the grass and watched it all, unseen and unsuspected, and he felt as if they were on the edge of the world, looking in and seeing everything, but untouched and untainted by it. Together they were a secret which had not yet been spoken, a book in which the words had been written but were still to be read. Above all, he felt the deep ties which joined him to the boy, the common purpose which bound their lives together in an unbreakable bond.

They left the field and walked along a road leading them back towards the city. There was one more place he wanted to take the boy, one more thing he had to make him understand. When they arrived at the gates, he felt the boy's fear shooting to the surface.

'It's all right, Samuel. Don't be frightened.'

But the boy stood motionless, reluctant to go any further.

'God's hand is on us now. Nothing can harm you or come close.'

He put his arm round the boy's shoulder and they entered side by side, the boy's body stiff under his touch. They walked between the long rows of headstones and he kept the boy close by his side. The path was strewn with the heads of withered flowers the wind had scattered. At the end of a row they stopped in front of a plot marked only by a metal number.

'This is my wife's grave. Five years ago I buried her here. I stood with my son just where we're standing now. There's something I want you to understand. This place where we're standing means nothing to me because she's not here. Only that body which suffered so much rests here, her soul has gone to be with her heavenly Father which is far better. The soul is what counts, Samuel, and nobody can harm the soul of those who are His through faith. My wife was a good woman and the Lord called her to be with Him. This world is not our real home, not for you and me, Samuel. Not for your father. Those men who killed your father couldn't kill his soul. Not the devil himself could do that.'

The boy stood still at his side, staring at the metal number. Spots of rain began to fall.

'"My beloved is gone down into His garden, to the beds of spices, to feed in the gardens and to gather lilies." That's what happened that day five years ago. He came down into His garden to gather lilies and He gathered Lorna and took her home. Some day I'll join her, just as some day you'll join your father. I brought you here because I want you to understand so that you can hold fast to the truth.'

Brown-edged petals swirled round their feet, and then were gone.

'Now I know you understand everything, we can go, and we don't ever have to come back here again, because here is just an empty grave; not here but risen.'

The boy followed him as he led the way out of the cemetery. Young trees strained at their stakes in the angry wind and his own coat billowed like a sail. As he pulled it tightly about him and lowered his head to his chest, a cortège of funeral cars drove past them, their windscreen wipers pushing aside the rain. The boy turned his face away and did not look.

HE COULD TELL that his mother was not sure about it. Despite the composure of her expression, she was weighing up all the factors in her head, itemising the different little bits of information into some kind of order before she reached a decision. The girl kept pushing her gently towards the decision she wanted.

'We'll take really good care of him, Mrs Anderson. Won't we, Billy?'

'Yeah, sure. He'll be as safe as houses. I have the car and he doesn't even have to get out of it if he doesn't want to. But if you're not happy – well, it's up to you.'

'It's very kind of you,' his mother said. 'It's just that I'm not sure . . .'

She hesitated, her hand flicking away hair that wasn't there. He watched her eyes examining the couple, taking in their clothes and their appearance, trying to gauge their characters and evaluate their degree of responsibility. She wasn't sure at all. He could see her eyes locking on the blond hair of the girl, the young man's leather jacket. But she was wavering.

'Maybe it would be good for Samuel to get out for a while. He'd enjoy seeing the bonfires and we wouldn't let him out of our sight for a second,' the girl said, smiling at her, her eyes wide with sincerity. 'It'd be a shame if he missed it.'

'Cindy, stop twisting Mrs Anderson's arm. Maybe she'd be happier if Samuel stayed here with her. It's only a bunch of fires. It's not the most exciting thing in the whole world.'

The reasonableness of the young man's words reassured his mother. He seemed a sensible boy, and if she didn't really know him very well, he was Mr Ellison's son. And if the girl's hair was too blond and out of a bottle, young people had their own styles and it was wrong to judge her. He sensed the thoughts flying about his mother's head like small birds. She looked at him with a question in her eyes.

'Would you like to go, Samuel?' she asked, the openness of her tone leaving the decision up to him.

He wanted to go. He wanted to see the great fires and as he nodded his head, the girl put her arm round his shoulders and the boy ruffled his hair. His mother smiled, her confidence that she had made the right decision beginning to rise.

'I suppose it'll be right and late before he's home,' she said.

'Well, some of the big fires don't get lit until midnight, but it all depends,' the girl replied.

His mother hesitated, but she had already committed

herself. He could see little bubbles of doubt floating to the surface.

'But it's only once a year, and it'd be a shame to miss it,' the girl insisted. 'Sure, Samuel could have a good lie on in the morning.'

His mother allowed herself to be persuaded, but the doubts still lingered in her eyes.

'There wouldn't be any trouble, would there?'

'No, no,' the young man answered. 'Just people having a bit of fun. There's nothing to worry about.'

His mother shelved her remaining objections and gave her permission, telling him to go upstairs and wrap up well. As he scampered up the stairs he could hear her explaining things to the couple, making sure they understood, giving them advice. When he returned his mother insisted on the young man taking five pounds, forcing it on him under the title of 'petrol money', then she turned back to him and checked his appearance, smoothing his hair with the palm of her hand.

'Maybe it'll be good for Samuel to get out without me hovering at his shoulder,' she said to no one in particular as she buttoned his jacket. 'We've been cooped up a lot in the house. Maybe a change will be good for him.'

As they drove off in the car he turned and waved through the rear window, telling her that he was all right and she was not to worry. The girl sat sideways on the front seat talking all the time, sometimes turning to smile at him and check that he was okay. His eyes examined her hair, her red-coloured lips. She laughed a lot and her words splashed about him like drops of water while her companion drove the car, seemingly indifferent to the constant stream of chatter, almost as if his thoughts were somewhere else. The car was old and it struggled as they drove further into the Castlereagh hills. He was unsure why they were heading upwards rather than down into the city, and as the engine dropped into lower gear on the steep climb it began to labour, with the heaving engine threatening to stall.

'We're going up here because you get a really good view of the city,' the girl explained.

'First time we ever came up here just to look at the view.'

'Hush, Billy,' she laughed, slapping his shoulder with the back of her hand. 'Don't you pay any attention to anything he says, Samuel. He just likes his wee jokes.'

The car groaned to the top of the hill and stopped at a metal gate into a field. They got out and sat on the top bar.

'Well, Samuel, what do you think of that?' she asked.

He stared down into the black basin of night, its glittering frost of light cold to his eyes, as cold as the metal bar under his hands. It was the same frozen picture he saw each night from his room. But then he looked again and this time he saw them – red embers of light sparking in the darkness like fireflies, tiny quivering glows of colour and faint grey palls of smoke mingling with the night sky. Billy began to point them out to him, telling him which parts of the city they belonged to, where the biggest fires were, about the rivalries which existed between different districts.

'Come on, Billy. I'm getting cold,' the girl said, climbing down awkwardly from the gate and brushing the seat of her jeans.

'Women, Samuel – they nag you to take them some-where, and when you get there, they want to go some-where else. You take my advice on women – give them a wide berth.'

'It's getting cold and we'll miss it if we don't go,' she insisted.

'Can't have Cindy getting cold, can we, Samuel?'

They clambered into the car and headed down into the east of the city. He felt safe in the car and a little excited, as they drove past streets where remnants of small fires continued to burn and crowds of people strolled along the pavements. Sometimes the crowds spilled into the road but he felt cut off from them, closed in his own little triangle of security. Often people waved at Billy and he shouted back bantering greetings. Someone sat on the bonnet before jumping off again. He realized that the crowds were beginning to move in the one direction. Many of them were drinking from cans of beer and he could hear bursts of discordant song, while in the back-ground throbbed the dull thud of insistent drumming. The smell of burning filtered into the car as the crush of people forced them to park and join the singing, dancing flow.

Usually he could not bear to be with crowds of people, but he felt as if these people were joined together in one face and it was a face which wished him no harm. The girl took him by the hand, making him feel like a child, but he let her lead him closer to where the great fire had started to blaze. The deep-throated crackle and spit of the fire blended with the reeling songs of the revellers, as the innards of the fire caught, shooting fierce tongues of flame up through the brittle tinder which hooped and sloped the narrowing sides to the sky. A streaming grey funnel of smoke spiralled above the terraced houses, lighting fires in their windows and dispersing fantails of smoke until they were swallowed by the blackness. He felt the growing heat on his face. The girl had let go of his hand now and she was drinking from a bottle someone had passed to her. When she was not drinking from it she jigged a little dance, circling herself and holding her free hand in the air. Billy stood sipping from a can of beer, quiet, pensive, at a distance from everything that went on around him.

Suddenly, the fire gave a loud bang as something exploded in the intensity of the heat and a cheer broke from the throat of the crowd. The noise startled him and gradually the sounds and colours of the night began to fuse, with reds and oranges, blue-tipped flames washing over everything, until everywhere he looked and everyone he saw was bathed in the savage glow of the fire. He wanted to pull further back from the flames, but the girl danced with more abandon, her movements exaggerated and uncoordinated. She was drinking more. Sometimes she stopped and hugged him, inviting him to join her, but he turned his head away. Billy smiled at him and went on sipping his beer. They stood for a long time, while the fire burned on, ravenous, self-consuming, and everywhere was washed by the red of the fire. Red like a setting sun. Red like rain bleeding across the sun. He shivered and a whorl of sickness unwound in his stomach. He screwed his eyes tightly shut, tried to deafen his ears, but the heat of the fire felt like it was searing his skin inch by inch. A hand rested on his shoulder.

'Are you all right, kid?'

He nodded a lie, but he knew he was still watching him. Then Billy dropped the beer can to the ground and called to Cindy, who had drifted over to some friends. He told her they were going. She looked surprised and confused.

'But Billy, it's only half gone. What's the rush?'

'We're taking Samuel home now. Come on,' he said with a sense of finality.

They started to make their way back across the waste ground towards the car, mixing with other groups who were beginning to drift away. She was complaining all the time, but he ignored her. The wail of a fire engine sliced the air. When they had almost reached the car, two men appeared and called to Billy by name. He spoke to them briefly then opened the car.

'I won't be long,' he said.

'Billy, where're you going?'

'Nowhere. Just a bit of business. It won't take long.'

She sat back sulkily in the front seat. Past her blond hair, through the front windscreen, he could see the remains of the fire shuddering its final desperate flames into the sky. The inside of the car swam with the orange light of a street lamp and the red glow from the fire, tiny reflections stuttering in the glass. Flickering in the glass like serpents of fire.

'He'll do this once too often. One day I'll not be sitting waiting for him when he comes back. Thinks he's God's gift to women – but he's not the only boy in the world.'

She took a brush out of her bag and angrily brushed

her hair with long, sweeping strokes, looking at herself
in her little vanity mirror. She saw him watching her.
The brushing seemed to drain her anger away and when
she had finished, she shook her hair gently and flounced
it with her hand. Then she turned sideways on the seat
and smiled at him.

'I'm sure you wouldn't treat your girlfriend like this.'

She knelt on the seat and turned fully round to face
him, her face framed by the fiery halo of light and her hair
tumbling over the top of the seat. A gold chain glinted at
her open neckline.

'Did you get a bit frightened at the fire? You did,
didn't you, you poor wee mite? But don't you worry
yourself, we're here to look after you.'

She leaned forward and patted him on the knee. He
could see the blue-veined tops of her breasts. She looked
at him with curious eyes.

'Why won't you talk, Samuel? Why don't you talk to
me? We could be friends, secret friends. You'd like that,
wouldn't you?'

He stared into her wide, persuasive eyes.

'Just you and me. No one else would know.'

The red light flickered on her face, deepening the
colour of her lips.

'Do you think I'm pretty, Samuel? Do you think
I've nice hair? Would you like to touch it? You would,
wouldn't you? Don't be frightened.'

She took his hand and placed it on her hair. His
hand froze on the blond curls.

Slowly, he opened his fingers and let them run through
her hair.

'That's better. You like that, don't you? Now, why don't you trust me and speak to me? Secret friends, that's what we'd be.'

She placed her finger gently on his lips.

'Why don't you use this tiny mouth of yours to speak to me? Don't be frightened. It would make us secret friends. Our secret and no one else's.'

He glanced up at her, then stared past the fire in her hair to where rain was bleeding across the sun. His hand dropped from her hair as if he had been burnt. But she put her finger under his chin and tilted his mouth upwards, then kissed it, pushing his lips open and filling him with the hot surge of her scent and the wine on her breath. He squirmed back into the seat. He was slipping into the fire, sinking into the flames. She drew back and smiled at him.

'Secret friends,' she whispered, as out of the shadows a figure strode towards the car.

'Well, that wasn't long, was it?' he asked.

'Long enough,' she complained, but her voice held only the pretence of anger.

'All right, Samuel?' he asked, looking at him in the rear view mirror.

'Oh, don't you worry about Samuel. We've been having a good talk. Just the two of us.'

'And what've you been talking about?'

'That's for us to know and you to find out,' she pouted.

The car started and they drove slowly home. At regular intervals they passed smouldering mounds of ash and coiled metal springs, which blistered the blackened ground.

THE GIRL HAD spent the night. He had heard her voice in the early hours of the morning and the front door closing as she slipped away. It was an abomination to him, bringing shame to his house and provoking a greater wrath than his. He could not let such sin come so close for fear it would infect the holiness of the task that had been appointed to him. He knew, too, that his son had committed other sins which warranted a much greater punishment. An image of the yellow parcel in the garage forced its way into his consciousness and made him shiver, but he tried to push it back into the dark sea. He closed his eyes and prayed that God would reveal to him what must be done.

Perhaps to balance the bitterness of the present, he often found his mind drifting into the warmth of the past, where his son was still a young child. There were good memories there for him and he lingered over them with affection, reluctant to exchange them for the husks of the present. He turned them over slowly, handling them delicately, almost frightened that they might fragment under his touch and vanish into the darkness. There was one which was special to him, precious not because of its drama or magnitude but because of its simple purity which warmed his soul. He remembered it all so clearly, remembered the scent of the day, even the clothes the three of them had worn. He had been working in a local park on a summer's afternoon, planting out a bedding display. He could still see the plants – lobelia, alyssum, salvia – feel the warmth of the soil on his fingers, the cool, smooth, wooden shaft of the spade. Looking up and seeing Lorna with the child in his pram, being surprised and pleased. Drinking the lemonade from the flask she had brought. Showing the boy off to the men with whom he worked. Feeling proud. Later he had taken the child to the swings and sat him on his mother's knee, and pushed gently. The light, careful push he gave the swing, the little squeals of protest when she felt she was going too high. The child's laughter.

The child's laughter. He clung desperately to its sound, trying to fight off the resurgence of the present, but it faded, a tiny diminishing echo into an unreachable past. He wondered where the years had gone, but was almost glad to find no answer – from their brittle deadness he could spark no flame, force no flicker of warmth or joy.

He wondered, too, how God could use such a life to bring about His will but then he heard the boy's voice speaking to him, reminding him again of the desert rock struck by God's power and from which flowed a gushing stream. The boy often spoke to him now, bringing him messages of truth and guiding him when he was confused about which direction to take. Perhaps the boy would help him now in his dealings with his son. Perhaps he would help him find the right words.

He went to the locked sideboard, opened it and brought out the ledgers. They squatted heavily on the table and he felt a reluctance to open them, even to touch them, but he knew it was the task which was appointed to him. He opened the top one, turning each page with a feeling of reverence and of foreboding. As always, he paused at the picture of the boy, tracing his outline with his fingers, peering close to read the writing, before moving on again. Already, two more pages had been filled with the names and pictures of those smitten by the great sickness. There was a new one to be added and he smoothed the morning paper flat before he began to cut with studied concentration. As he was finishing it, his son entered the room, barefoot, unwashed, and slumped onto the settee, then glanced over at the clock to see what time of day it was. Neither spoke for some time. He pasted the picture onto the page and sat staring it into his consciousness.

'You'd no right to bring that girl home here last night.'

'Her name's Cindy. It wouldn't kill you to use it sometimes.'

'I can think of another name for her.'

'What's that supposed to mean?'

'I know she stayed all night. Stayed here right under this roof.'

'So what if she did, Da? It's not the end of the world. It was late when we got in, by the time we left the boy home . . . You don't begrudge her a roof over her head, do you?'

'That's not why she stayed. And if you've no thought for your own soul have some thought for hers.'

He slammed the picture flat with the palm of his hand.

'I live here too, Da. I pay my way – that gives me rights too.'

'It doesn't give you the right to fly in the face of God's law, to bring shame to this house.'

'No one's brought shame to anyone. The only shame's inside your head. When are you going to start living in the real world, Da?'

'Live in your world, you mean. "We are of this world but not part of it."'

'If you're going to start quoting the Bible, I'm not going to go on talking to you. Why, just once, can't you speak to me in your own words without coming out with all that stuff?'

'They're not my words, William. They're God's, and if you hadn't hardened your heart you would listen to them now and know the truth of them.'

He saw his son's face darken with anger.

'Hardened my heart? I haven't hardened my heart. I have feelings here, feelings you'll never know about. And you're a good one to be talking about hearts. What feelings did you ever have in your heart when you used to beat the hell out of me with the belt? Whose heart was hard, Da, when you used to take me and belt me till your arm was sore?'

'I never laid a hand on you but I did it in love – did it because I cared about you.'

'And because you beat me in love, do you think that made the pain any less, made the welts go away any sooner?'

He watched his son pull his knees up to his chest, hug

himself against the memory. He turned his gaze back to the open ledger, unsure of what to say, unable to make him understand. It had always been like this, as long as he could remember. Maybe he was right – maybe he had been too hard, his hand too heavy, but he had done it in love. Whatever the boy thought, he had done it in love. He still felt that love now, but nothing he could say or do seemed capable of reaching him or touching any part of him. Now his son scoffed, mocked the things that were dear to him, and behind the laughter was a bitterness and an anger that corroded both their souls. He felt it reaching out to him now.

'And another thing, Da. What is it with these friggin' books that you spend half your life sticking those pictures in them? Are you running your own personal obituary column or something? If you are, you'll need a right few more books before this thing's over.'

He watched him laugh and light a cigarette, but he could see a genuine curiosity in his eyes.

'I record the dead. God has told me to do it. I record them here, all those smitten by the disease, the names of the innocent and the forgotten, all those swept into the pit.'

'God told you to do this?' His son's voice was raised in incredulity. 'God told you to do this? Do you not think, Da, that sometimes that voice you hear is not God's, but your own?'

He shook his head slowly in reply and closed the ledger.

'There was nothing innocent either about that last boy's photo you've just stuck in. He was up to his neck in it.'

'How do you know that?'

'It's known. They like to say it was random, sectarian, but he was one of theirs all right.'

He looked closely at his son, searching his face as he had those in the ledger.

'But how do you know?'

'I heard it, Da. I heard it from people who know. That's all, all right?'

'And maybe the people who know, know, too, who killed him.'

'Maybe they do and maybe they don't. I don't know anything about that. I mind my own business and you should, too.'

He watched him draw heavily on the cigarette, stub it out in the ash-tray balanced on the arm of the settee, then slouch into the kitchen. There was the sound of the kettle being filled and then his voice again.

'Smitten by the disease – that's a new name for a head job. I must remember that one.'

'It's a pity you didn't remember to bring the boy home sooner last night than you did. I'm sure his mother was worried about him. You should never've taken him anyway, letting him see a bunch of drunken people making fools of themselves.'

'We took him to see the bonfires. What's wrong with that? The kid needs all the help he can get.'

He returned from the kitchen carrying a cup of tea and sat down on the settee again.

'Never spoke a word all evening. Nothing. Just stared at the fire as if he saw a ghost in it.'

'The boy will speak when the time is right. God has

a reason and a purpose for all things. He works His will in His own time and in His own way.'

'Everything shitty that happens in the world, you say is God's will. How can you keep on saying it? It's a great way to avoid having to face up to anything. I don't even think you really believe it deep down. It's just something you say over and over, like some kind of tape recording.'

'I do believe it, William. I believe it with all my heart and you should too. Heaven . . .'.

'Heaven! There might be a God in your heaven, Da, making plans for everyone, but all that's in my heaven is space satellites and bits of junk going round and round until they burn up and fall to earth. That's all's in heaven.'

He watched his son's eyes flood with anger.

'I pray for you, William, and I'll keep on praying for you, hoping that some day you'll open your heart to the truth. I'm only glad your mother isn't here to hear you talk this way.'

'My mother,' he said, his voice breaking in bitterness. 'Don't talk to me about my mother, because I loved her. Loved her like you could never have if you accept what happened to her. I stopped believing in your God the months I stood holding her hand and watching her body being eaten away inch by inch. And when she died, I was gladder than I've ever been in my whole life, and you know something, Da, the day she died I cursed your God. What do you think of that, Da? I cursed your God.'

His son was standing up now, and the cup of tea had fallen from the settee onto the floor, and a little wisp of steam was rising as it soaked into the carpet. He was standing, and for a second he thought he was crying, but then he waved his hand dismissively in the air as if more words were a waste of time, and went back upstairs. He sat, watching the steam rising from the floor.

The light, careful push he gave the swing, the little squeals of protest when she felt she was going too high. The child's laughter. He stopped pushing, went and stood in front of the swing. As mother and child came towards him, he opened his arms to them both, their eyes warm with smiles, laughing as the downward motion of the swing carried them away again. The sweet scent of the day. All gone now, into the past.

He picked the cup off the floor, took it to the kitchen, then returned and mopped up the spill with a damp cloth. As he knelt mopping, he whispered into the silence, 'I loved her too', but the words had nowhere to go and they returned to him unheard, before vanishing for ever.

HE SAT IN the front passenger's seat of the car and watched Billy carefully. He was steering the car lightly with one hand, his elbow propped at a right angle against the open window. He studied him intently and then raised his own elbow to the same position. Billy's eyes flickered constantly from the road ahead to the pavements and side streets they were passing and sometimes he pushed a hand through his hair as he glanced at himself in the mirror. He wanted to try that too, but he contented himself by cataloguing it in his memory with all of Billy's other gestures. He liked being with Billy. He was the one person he knew whose life felt strong and sure of itself, and when Billy spoke he sounded as if there was nothing in the world which could ever frighten him. Sometimes he wished he could be more like Billy, learn the secret of his strength, and when he was with him he felt protected and sheltered by his indifference to anything which existed outside his own desires. Although he did not see him very often, he had begun to think that if he could somehow join his life to

Billy's, like a feather grafted onto a wing, he might be able to share enough of his strength to escape from his present world.

The car moved steadily along roads which were unfamiliar to him, responding smoothly to the driver's light one-handed touch. Watching him drive made him think that Billy was able to control everything which was part of his experience, coolly steering an unworried course in whatever direction his impulses took and always he seemed to hold himself at a safe distance from life. Just like the night when the flames had pulled everyone else into the fire, he had held himself apart and untouched. Perhaps if he watched Billy closely enough, spent more time with him, he might be able to share the secret of this strength.

They passed a group of young people standing outside a video shop. Billy sounded the horn as he passed them and they shot their arms into the air in salute, their heads angled to watch the disappearing car. A light rain was beginning to fall, darkening the pavements and turning the world grey. Only the neon signs of fast-food shops shone brightly in the falling gloom. It didn't feel like summer, at least not the ones which existed in his memory, and the strangeness of his surroundings made the world seem separate from season or time. He knew that by now the swallows would have left the farm, having gathered in great shifting shapes ready to make their long journey. The car's wipers pushed the rain aside and Billy glanced at him almost as if he had momentarily forgotten that he had a companion.

'Well, boss, you've my head turned the way you blether

on non-stop. You're a real motor-mouth. Can you not give my head peace for five minutes?'

Then he glanced away again as he studied a teenage girl waiting to cross the road.

'Put your window down and ask her if she wants a lift. A smooth-talking man like you could touch for any woman he wants.'

He sounded the horn as they passed her and laughed as the girl responded with a two-fingered gesture.

'Did you have a girlfriend back home, Sam boy? I bet a good-looking boy like you had a whole army of them – good country girls with big red cheeks and bits of straw in their hair.'

Leaning across from the driver's seat he ruffled the boy's hair. When he had finished and returned his attention to the road ahead, the boy waited a few seconds then pushed his hand back through his hair as he had watched Billy do. He had never had many friends, maybe because they lived quite far from other families, maybe because he was the type of person whom people did not want as their friend. He did not know the reason, but he wondered if Billy would become his friend.

'Ah, you're just right. Women are nothing but trouble. Look at me with Cindy hanging round my neck like a ball and chain. Give them a sideways look and they think they own your whole life. Talking about women – let's get our story right for your ma. Think hard, where'll we tell her we've been tonight? Good idea – the zoo. Now that's what I call thinking.'

His father had been the closest he had had to a friend. Even as a small child his father had let him accompany him in his work round the farm, taking time to explain things, showing him how things worked. In his memory he felt the rough weight of his father's guiding hand on his shoulder as he let his son steer his precious tractor, the heavy pat which wordlessly signalled his satisfaction when the short journey was safely completed. His father was mostly a quiet man but he could always tell what he was feeling by the expression on his face or the posture of his body. Sometimes when he read anger or a bad mood on his father's face he kept his distance and was careful not to get in his way, but such times never lasted more than a day or so and then they were brushed aside without reference or comment.

The rain had stopped now and Billy was singing a song about going to the zoo, making stupid animal noises and using his free arm to do impressions. Sometimes he nudged him in the ribs with his elbow as if encouraging him to join in. There was something bad between Billy and his father, but he did not know what it was or why it should be so. He remembered the old man saying that he had hoped Billy would be his helpmate but now it was not to be. He did not understand what the old man meant by a helpmate but he supposed it was something like the way he had helped his father on the farm. He listened to Billy making animal noises and wondered if anything bad would ever have come between him and his father, but he found it hard to imagine any future beyond that summer night, and as his thoughts began to circle round that moment, he too made animal noises inside his head and watched the world pass outside the car.

At first Belfast had seemed very big to him but he

saw now that it was a place with only a small number of faces which were repeated again and again. He didn't know where they were now, but gradually he became aware from the words and colours sprayed across walls that they had entered territory which was dangerous for them. He sank lower into the seat and suddenly he was aware that Billy had stopped singing. Despite the gloom he had pushed the sun visor down and then in the silence there was a distinct clicking noise as he locked the driver's door and told him to do the same. They had turned off a main road and were moving quite slowly through the tight network of backstreets, Billy driving now with both hands on the wheel and his eyes darting from house to house, scanning each passing face. It was as if he was looking for something or someone, but the car kept moving and when another car came towards them he turned his head away until it had passed. At some houses young children sat on doorsteps or chalked on the pavements and behind them open living-room doors revealed the foot of stairs and the flickering shadows of television sets. On one street corner a group of four men huddled in a little circle and some of them turned to scrutinize the approaching car, their eyes narrow with concentration. He heard Billy swear softly and then saw him suddenly raise a hand in an elaborate gesture of greeting. One of the group responded instinctively but they continued to stare at the car for a few seconds before returning to their conversation. As the car moved forward a little quicker Billy glanced repeatedly into his rear-view mirror until they turned into a new street and the men were left behind.

He hoped Billy would drive to safety but instead they

stopped on the edge of waste ground, the car's engine still
running. Some boys were playing handball against a gable
wall, while others were throwing stones at an old paint
tin, their direct hits making it jump and jerk. A small
girl rode by, close to the front of the car, the wheels
of her bicycle a fluorescent pink. Billy was studying a
row of houses, identical except for the colour of their
front doors. Occasionally one of the doors opened and
someone went in or out but there was little else to be
seen. A dog sniffed round the edge of a rain-filled pothole
and two boys wheeled a tyre almost as big as themselves
to some unknown destination.

'There's nothing to worry about, Samuel. We're going
in a minute – I just have to check out a couple of wee
things, that's all.'

He leaned forward and switched on the radio, drumming his fingers on the steering wheel in rhythm to the
music but occasionally his eyes still furtively checked the
mirror.

'Don't forget, now – we went to the zoo to see the
animals. But we won't be telling lies either because there's
more animals living here than there are in Bellevue, only
these ones are breeding faster.'

Smiling at his own joke he gave a final glance towards
the row of houses, put the car into gear and as they drove
away the feeling of danger receded street by street. Billy
wound his window down and propped his elbow on the
ledge again, and now when he looked in the mirror it
was only to study his reflection. Eventually the car took
them back to parts of the city he recognized and he sat up
straighter in his seat and watched Billy drive.

'Some day, kid, we'll get you a set of wheels and I'll teach you to drive. Something that goes a bit faster than a tractor. Then you can drive me around.'

They passed narrow streets where the houses on opposite sides were linked by lines of bunting and the kerbstones were painted in the same colours. Billy turned the radio louder and bounced on the seat as if he was sitting on a horse. Once, as a joke, he took his hand off the wheel for a second and covered his eyes, but it wasn't frightening because he felt safe with Billy and he knew they were not going to crash.

'Thirsty work, kid. Time for you and me to have a drink before I take you home.'

They parked in a side street outside what Billy called 'the club' – a building without windows or a name, faced only with grey plaster. There was a small camera above the metal door and an intercom into which Billy spoke before a buzzer sounded and he pushed the door open. A doorman greeted Billy with a smile and a pat on the back and when they entered the crowded lounge he was surprised by how plush and comfortable everything looked, despite the smell of smoke and alcohol. There were fruit machines ranged along one wall and a couple of blue-baized pool tables. To the side of the bar was a wide television screen and above it pictures of the Queen and football teams. On a side wall hung some sort of memorial plaque with a Latin inscription. Everyone in the club seemed to know Billy and he joked with them and took playful sips out of their drinks. He watched Billy as he approached a table in a corner of the room where half a dozen men sat in some sort of discussion that seemed to separate them from the people around them. He saw Billy point to him but could not hear what was said, and then he was called over to the table and introduced by Billy as his 'mate'. Some of the men shook his hand. One of them had tattoos completely covering his arms and called him 'big lad'. An orange juice and a packet of crisps arrived from the bar for him and he was given a seat at the table. The men were older than Billy and when he started to talk about where he had just been, one of them stopped him sharply, his speech studded with swear words. Billy reddened and said something about it being safe to talk in front of the boy but the man shook his head and stopped any further discussion. A waiter came and cleared the accumulated debris of bottles and glasses, examining them carefully to check that they were empty before he placed them quickly and neatly on his tray.

'Jackie, give the kid a game of pool,' said the man who had sworn at Billy, 'and get him another drink or something.'

The man who stood up was the one with the tattoos on his arms and as he led the way to the pool table he walked with a limp. They went to a table where two youths were playing and Jackie leaned across the table, lifted the cue ball and smiled at the two players. Without any words being exchanged, they placed their cues on the table and walked away. Another glass of orange arrived from the bar and they played two games of pool, but he knew that Jackie was missing shots deliberately and over-praising him when he managed to pocket a ball. Once when he fluked a shot, his opponent turned to him with wide eyes and mock amazement.

'Big lad, you're a bit of a Hurricane Higgins. What's

in that orange juice you're drinking? I'll have to start drinking it and give up the beer.'

As the man bent down to play his shot Samuel could see part of a spider's web tattoo appear at the top of his chest while across one set of knuckles were the blue letters which spelt HATE and across the other, the word LOVE.

'You're a bit of a hustler, kid. I'm not playing you for a fiver. Hey, boss, cat got your tongue?'

He looked around for Billy, but he was part now of the tightly knit group in the corner and the only sounds he could hear were the click of the pool balls and the clink of glasses. Their table sat like a little island and none of the tide of activity which filled the rest of the club seemed to flow round it.

'You're just friggin' right, son. It's the best way nowadays. See no evil, speak no evil – that's the safest way to be. Look at me – my mouth's what got me this,' he said, pointing to his leg with the pool cue.

Then he put the cue under his arm like a crutch and hopped round the table doing an impersonation of Long John Silver. When he had finished his performance they started to play another game but Billy arrived and said it was time to go. The man with the tattoos pretended he was relieved.

'Aye, take him home, Billy. The kid's a hustler, never gave me a look-in. Whipped the pants off me.'

He leaned once more on his pretend crutch and winked at Billy and as they left the club other people shouted goodbye and raised their glasses. The doorman got off his stool and opened the door for them, offering a tip for a horse which he described as a 'dead cert', but Billy just laughed and led the way back to where the car was parked.

'Geordie wouldn't know a dead cert if it ran him over,' he said as he started the car's engine.

As he watched Billy smiling he smiled too, and in that shared moment he felt that some of Billy's strength had started to reach out and touch him. He leaned back in the passenger's seat and thought that if only he could carefully plant his steps in Billy's firm footprints he might be able one day to stand where he now stood. Like a game he used to play with his father on the beach – echoing his steps, with legs stretched wide and stiff like compasses to match his stride, leaving no trail of his own as he followed the predetermined path. With a tiny tremor of pride he remembered, too, the way the men had shaken his hand and he realized for the first time that through his father's death he had become someone important – someone people felt sorry for. As the car cruised the empty roads he wondered how long it would last, but as they got closer to home his calculations of self-pity were replaced by the sharp sting of shame.

HE FOLLOWED AT a safe distance, sheltering in shop doorways when they stopped. The crowded city centre afforded him protection from discovery and he was able to stay close enough to the boy and his mother to catch every expression which crossed their faces. The very sight of the boy gave him pleasure, reassured his insecurities and confirmed his future course. He watched them as they studied a window display, oblivious to his presence. She was pointing out things to him and he was nodding his head in response, but he knew that for the boy the objects were meaningless things, the worthless debris which misguided people spent their lives accumulating, only to realize too late that they brought nothing but misery. He loved the boy more each day and gave constant thanks for the gift of his coming. He had waited a long time, longer than he could bear to remember, and there had been times when despair had almost destroyed his faith, but now the moment had almost come. He felt the full force of its inevitability as their two lives converged towards it and it filled him with expectancy.

He glanced around him, looked into the faces streaming past him and in every face he saw the signs of the sickness, but no longer did his spirit feel crushed by sorrow because he knew that soon each one of them could reach out and find healing if only they would look in faith. He never let himself think about what it would be like when the healing came because no matter how hard he tried it was beyond his imagination, the pictures he tried to create in his mind always blocked out by images of the present. But it was so very close now, closer than any of these people filling the city street would ever realize. The boy knew though. He could see the readiness in his face, read his anticipation in every movement of his body, and as he watched him he had to struggle to prevent himself from reaching out to him and gathering him in his arms. Separated from the boy he felt incomplete, vulnerable in his isolation and inadequacy.

He followed them into a large store, nervous when the flow of shoppers broke his eye contact, watching as the boy and his mother drifted apart, each pursuing their own interests. The boy was standing in front of banked rows of television sets and videos, most of the screens showing the same cartoons in a frenetic flicker of bright pinks and blues. Pop music was playing loudly in the background. The boy stood very still, his eyes seemingly locked to the wall of screens, his slight frame almost inconspicuous in the crowded store. Only his red hair stopped him from being lost in the hustling crowds. The electric glow of the television sets washed over his pale moon face, infusing it with a changing transfer of colour, only the red of his hair untouched and unaltered.

'Hello, Mr Ellison, out doing a bit of shopping?'

As he spun round his arm knocked over some video tapes, clattering them to the floor. He watched as she knelt down to pick them up.

'I hope I didn't startle you. The noise in these places is terrible. I don't know how the assistants can stick it all day.'

She was looking at him, waiting for some response, but he was still confused and could not think what to say. He helped her tidy the tapes back into their original position.

'It's very warm too. I suppose it must be all the lights and equipment.'

'It is very warm, Mrs Anderson.'

'Shops have changed a lot since my day. You know, I hardly recognize the city centre. There's not many of the old stores left now, and everything seems to be geared to teenagers.'

He nodded his head vaguely as she spoke, unsure of what he was agreeing to.

'Samuel's over there, watching something on television.'

She pointed in the boy's direction while he smiled at her and nodded again. He had to regain control of himself, give her no cause for suspicion. Soon enough she would understand, reap her own reward for the work her son was about to do.

He talked with her for a few minutes and then the conversation stumbled into silence. He could see that she was about to go, but suddenly she hesitated and turned to him again.

'Mr Ellison, I'm a bit worried about Samuel. You've spent a lot of time with him recently. Do you see any signs of him getting better? I'm just not sure anymore.'

He reached out and touched her gently on the arm. He wanted to tell her, he wanted so much to tell her, but knew he could not.

'The boy will be all right if you have the faith to believe it. Soon he will be well again.'

He could see that she wanted to believe him, tell that his words brought her comfort and a moment later, as she thanked him, he smiled at her. She was a good woman. He watched her as she made her way towards the boy and he was glad that soon God would take away the pain of her grief. He would leave them now. It would be foolish to take the risk of being seen again, and with a final lingering look at the boy, he went out into the city streets. He found himself in a square where various groups and speakers assailed the passing crowds with their different messages. Their voices shouted shrilly in a cacophonous competition as they urged their particular brand of false salvation on the indifferent passers-by, but he was not angered by the sight of these false prophets, but instead was struck by the terrible futility of what they did. It was as if each one was building a miserable little Tower of Babel, each speaking a language that no one else understood. The higher their voices soared, the more people seemed to speed on their way, barely turning their heads to give them a fleeting glance.

He was growing tired and knew it was time to return home but first, on impulse, he went into a shop selling everything to do with gardening. He examined the rows of garden tools, handling spades and garden forks as if testing their balance and weight, then perused packets of seed, holding the coloured pictures of flowers close to his face. He bought a packet, even though he knew it would mean waiting for spring before he could sow them. It was a small pleasure he could look forward to and the boy would be able to help him. No matter how he thought of the future now, he always pictured it with the boy by his side and on the bus which took him home, his hand played with the packet of seed, rattling it gently in his pocket.

There was a strange car parked outside his house. At first, he assumed it was something to do with his son, but as he got closer he recognized the man sitting in it. As he drew level with it, the man got out, and after locking the car door, came round to greet him with his hand extended.

'Hello, Henry, how are you? It's been a bit of a while.'

As he shook the outstretched hand he looked into the man's eyes with curiosity. It had been a long time – maybe a couple of years since they had last met. He wondered what had brought him. Under the high-necked woollen jumper he could see the green collar of his policeman's shirt and when he glanced down, a pair of shiny black boots under faded cord trousers.

'I'm fine John, and how are you?'

'Struggling on, struggling on. I'm just finishing a shift and I thought I'd call up and see you.'

There was a moment of silence, and he knew his caller did not want to talk in the street. He nodded and invited him into the house, his fingers fumbling with the front door key. He could feel the man watching him and it made him nervous and clumsy in his movements. The offer of a cup of tea was accepted and as he stood in the kitchen getting things ready, he could sense the contents of his living-room being explored. He tried to hurry, but the kettle seemed to take a long time to boil.

'How's your family doing, John?' he asked, unsure of how many children his visitor now had.

'Not too bad, thanks. Gail's still working part-time in the bank. I think it gets her out of the house more than anything else. And the oldest boy did his exams in June. One minute they're a nipper and the next they're learning to drive. And Diane, the youngest, she's starting her new school in September. The uniform alone must've cost a week's pay.'

He carried the two cups of tea through to the living-room where the man was leaning back on the settee in a too-forced posture of ease. As he carefully handed over the hot cup, their eyes met briefly before each looked away.

'And you, Henry. How's life treating you? You're looking well enough.'

'I'm doing fine. Sometimes I get a bit tired, that's all, but I suppose at my age I can't complain about that.'

'Sure we all suffer from that complaint. I see you're keeping yourself busy. The old garden's looking as well as ever.'

'Aye, I still take an interest in it. It keeps me busy and I give a bit of a hand with next door's.'

'I must get you round to throw your eye over ours. What with Gail and myself out mostly, it's got itself into a bit of a mess. Maybe you could give us some advice on what to do with it.'

He nodded noncommittally but said nothing.

'And what about William? What's he doing with himself now?'

He held his cup carefully to his lips and searched for the right words.

'The last time I spoke to you, you were telling me he was doing some sort of course at the Tech, isn't that right?'

'He never finished it. He dropped out half-way through.'

'That's a pity. He always was a bit of a restless spirit.'

A thin silence froze over the moment as they both drank from their cups and watched each other. But there was to be no respite.

'And what's he doing now?'

'A bit of this and a bit of that. Nothing very regular. You know what young people are like. He's interested in cars.'

'Aye, I do indeed. I'm sorry to hear he's not settled yet. Maybe something'll turn up soon. I could keep my ear to the ground for him if you like. You say he's interested in cars?'

'William's always followed his own course. He doesn't tell me much about what he does. I suppose we don't always get on the best.'

'That's the way of the world now. I know you always did your best by the boy.'

There was a silence longer than any of the others and then as the man opposite leaned forward towards him, he knew he was about to learn the reason for his visit. He grew tense, a little frightened and flustered to his feet, trying to postpone whatever it was that was coming.

'Would you like some more tea John? There's plenty in the pot.'

'No, you're all right, thanks. I know you're wondering why I've come, and if it was just a social visit it would be a bit late in the day. I've been a bit neglectful in that respect, but I'm still mindful of the help you and Lorna gave me when I needed it, and I suppose that's the reason why I'm here now.'

He paused and set his cup on the floor beside his feet.

'It's about William, Henry. I've heard his name mentioned in the station. Nothing specific now, but mentioned all the same. He's running with a bad crowd and if he keeps on running with them he'll end up in trouble. Could be big trouble too, by the sound of it. I'm telling you this because I owe you. Maybe you could talk to him, scare him off, or if you like I could maybe speak to him.'

'You say a bad crowd –'

'People that are dangerous to be around. Some with records, and some clever enough to get others to do their dirty work. But all of them bad news and the boy would be best far away from them – far away before it's too late.'

'I'm grateful to you, John, for telling me this, and I'll talk to him like you say, make him see some sense. Maybe he'll find a decent job soon and leave all this behind him. Don't worry – I'll talk to him all right, get him to see the mess he's getting himself into.'

He said all the things he thought would sound convincing, but behind his words was a small feeling of relief that there had been no worse to tell. His son's name had been mentioned – that was the extent of it. Perhaps it was destined to go no further than that, perhaps he really would try once more to reach him. They talked on, their conversation slowly drifting into shared memories of the past, but as they talked he knew he could trust no one but the boy who had been given to him. Gradually the talk returned to the present and he found his thoughts turning towards the ledgers.

'We live in godless times, John. I suppose in your job you know that better than anybody.'

'I've seen a few things I could've done without, but I suppose, though, I've been luckier than most. But I mustn't keep you any longer, Henry. I'm sorry it took me so long to getting round to see you, and I'm just sorry that when I did, it was to bring you bad news.'

'I'm grateful to you – I know you didn't have to come.'

As his visitor opened the front door he noticed the band of indentation his cap had pressed into his hair. He stopped in the driveway and looked at the garden.

'I'll have to give you a shout and see what you can suggest for my square of jungle.'

'That man who was killed the other night was a bad business – the one whose body was found in the quarry.'

'It was that, and not the first one to be dumped there either. You always keep it very neat.'

'They claimed he was involved. Do you think that was true?'

'I don't rightly know. From what I heard he was just another nobody who had the misfortune to be in the wrong place at the wrong time. Mostly that's the case – just some punter whose luck has run out.'

He took one last glance at the garden, then said his goodbyes and got into his car. As he stood watching the car disappear into the distance, his hand felt the packet of seed, and walking back to the house he opened it and let the seed run through his fingers like grains of sand.

AS EACH DAY went by he could feel the frayed fabric of their lives slowly unravel, and it frightened him because he did not know where or how it would end. Each day, too, whatever it was that held his mother's life together loosened a little, and she lost more of the solid strength which he had always identified with her. She had brought them both to Belfast because she had thought it might be a new start, but although she would not admit it openly, it had been a mistake. Back home were bad memories, but they had not lessened their grip by moving away. They had left behind only what was familiar and replaced it with what was strange and unsettling. His mother had believed she was returning to somewhere which would be like an old friend, but everything had changed and the city she once knew existed only in her memory. She had talked of taking a job but he saw no sign of her trying to find one, and they found themselves living from day to day in a nowhere world which was without shape or purpose.

His mother cleaned the house incessantly, often at

strange hours of the day, and grew irritable if he left his possessions anywhere but in their proper place. Sometimes when he woke in the middle of the night he would hear the whirr of the washing machine or the sullen drone of the vacuum cleaner, searching out new breeding grounds for dust and dirt. Sometimes, too, when he came upon her unexpectedly, he knew she had been crying and although she would try to disguise it he could always tell. She still wore a public mask of resilience which she was too proud to let slip, and when relations called they always expressed admiration for how well she was coping, but he knew she was deceiving them. It was a little show she put on for their visits and it faded with their departure.

After a while the visits decreased in regularity and it was obvious that she was glad, resenting the intrusion into her privacy. The visits were always the same – polite cups of tea, meaningless talk and embarrassed silences; conversations that skirted round everything sensitive and dangerous, and only feelings of relief when the visits were over. Even those relations she had once spoken of with affection now seemed to produce only indifference and occasional annoyance.

The one thing which helped him a little was the work in the garden which, with the old man's guidance, they were gradually reclaiming from its original wilderness. They spent a couple of hours most days, often longer, weeding and digging out new flower beds. A couple of times his mother helped too. He put a lot of energy into the work and sometimes he was able to lock his mind into a mechanical routine which numbed his feelings and thoughts. The old man remained a mystery to which he could find no sure answer, but now there were many parts of his life for which no meaning existed. Often his words made no sense and mostly they drifted through his senses like clouds, before disappearing into some distant void. The old man talked of God a lot and how God had some kind of plan in which they were both to play a part but he could not understand how this could be. In his own heart he hated God and knew that God returned his hatred, and yet he did not believe that what had happened had done so by chance. God had allowed it to happen – he did not know why, but the more he thought of it all, the more he knew it was so. Perhaps, after all, it really was some sort of plan – even though his father never did harm to anyone – which might some day be explained to him. Like all the others the old man talked of healing, told him that God could take away the fear that clutched at his heart, take away the pain of his mother's grief, but if God did not care enough to do a little thing to save his father why, then, should He do this now?

As they worked in the garden, he glanced up at the old man and watched him turning over the soil with his spade. It glinted with dampness and a worm slithered slowly through it, seeking new shelter. The old man did not see him watching, and his tongue lolled out from the side of his mouth as he raised the spade in the air and wielded it like an axe to split some sods of earth. The old man could go on believing in God if he wanted to, but some day he too would find that God didn't care. As the old man pushed his boot down on the lug of the spade a sole of caked earth fell from his boot and crumbled into the turned soil.

They were spending more time together. His mother encouraged it. Even at home he'd never had many friends. Now there was little else to do. His mother didn't go out much and made jobs for herself in the house, manufacturing increasingly meaningless tasks which were designed to consume her time and restlessness.

When the old man decided that they had finished their work for the day they carried his tools through a gap in the hedge and stored them in the garage. He watched the care with which the old man shut and locked the door, and assumed he was frightened that someone might steal the tools, because there was nothing else of any value to be seen. As he turned to go back to his own garden he felt a hand on his shoulder, leading him back. He had never been in the old man's house before, but he followed him with a growing sense of curiosity, staring up at the lifeless windows which reflected nothing but their own emptiness.

Billy was sitting in the kitchen, slumped forward on the table, his head surrounded by uncleared plates. The radio was on and a man was reading the news, reciting new names and places of death. As they came in, he raised his head sharply as if startled, and wiped his mouth with the back of his hand.

'Hi, kid. What about you?'

The old man ushered him into the living-room as if his son had not spoken. The voice from the radio followed them, seeking to push its way inside his head but he barred it out with practised skill, trying to concentrate only on what he could see, cataloguing everything in the room with deliberate exactitude. There was a faint musty

smell lingering over the furniture which looked old and
shabby as if it had reached the end of its life. There was
no sign of anything new or bright. The fire was almost
dead and everywhere there was an air of neglect. He
pictured his mother being let loose in it and the welcome
challenge it would present to her. If allowed, she could
find enough cleaning to keep her occupied for a long time
and be spared the frustration of having to search for new
things to do. Perhaps she might take it on in return for
the old man's work in the garden, but the more he looked
about, the more he sensed that he was standing close to
some secret which would not welcome prying eyes or a
stranger's hand. He felt it all about him, unspoken words
and hidden memories, which lurked behind the faded wallpaper and threadbare furniture, and although he wasn't
sure, he did not think that they were good memories. On
a wall was a black and white wedding photograph of a
young man with a nervous face standing stiffly in a square-
shouldered suit. It was difficult to see the small face of the
bride as it seemed almost shadowed by the flouncing veil.

The old man sat down at the table and gestured to
him to do the same. For the first time, he noticed the
green ledgers. The old man was looking at them too.
The voice from the radio slipped momentarily through
the barrier he had erected, but then seeped away again.
He wondered what was in the books but the old man
continued to stare intently and said nothing. The radio
voice was replaced by music. A woman was singing
about love. The old man stretched out his hand and
placed it palm down on the cover of the top book.

'They're here,' he said. 'The names of the dead. I record

them all – since the very start, before you were even born. Many names. But not for much longer, because we're very close to the moment when it will begin. Every day brings us closer to it.'

The old man was talking to him but still staring at the books, almost as if his words were directed to them. He wondered if his father's name was there. The old man spoke more and more about healing, but the spider writing on the walls and the voices from radio and television spoke only of more deaths. Sometimes when the old man talked like this it felt as though he was talking only to himself, trying to hold onto some strange dream which had no meaning.

After a while the old man stood up from the table and without speaking left the room. His departure brought a new silence to it, and the voice on the radio grew louder. He heard the old man's footsteps in the room above and the sound of a toilet flushing. Then, suddenly, he knew that someone was watching him and he turned sharply to see Billy standing in the doorway. They smiled at each other. He came over to the table and sat down on the chair beside him, winking at him and then raising his eyes in the direction of the ceiling.

'Don't pay too much heed, kid, to what ma da comes out with. His head's full of slamming doors. He's getting old and sometimes things get mixed up in his head. Just listen, don't pay it any heed.'

He watched Billy's face break into a smile.

'Just listen – that's a good one. You never do anything else, do you, kid? Tell me this. What do you do with all the words that people pour into that head of yours? If you've any sense, you'll not store them up but let them in one ear and out the other. I've been doing that all my life with ma da. And at the end of the day, words aren't worth shit. Just nod – that's all the encouragement he needs.'

Billy's eyes rested on the ledgers.

'What's he doing with these out? He's not thinking of showing you those, is he? God in Heaven, he's not doing his bit about recording the dead. Other old lads keep scrapbooks, but they put postcards or stamps in them, not bloody obituaries!'

As he spoke, he laughed and shook his head from side to side.

'Cutting out bits of newspaper isn't going to stop this thing – but you know that better than anyone. There's only one way'll end this and it's their way.' He could hear the old man's heavy footsteps on the stair. 'It took us a long time to learn the lesson, but we understand it now, kid. "Our day will come" – that's their cry, but their day has come and gone and now it's time to pay them back, time to settle the score.'

Billy stretched out his hand and rested it on his shoulder.

'Time to pay them back for your father, Samuel.'

He looked into Billy's eyes for a second then turned away from the intensity which burned there. As the old man entered the room Billy stood up and the hand which had been resting on his shoulder playfully ruffled his hair. He glanced again at Billy's face but the fire had gone, replaced by a familiar smile.

'Believe it, kid. It's coming soon.'

The old man looked at them both, anxious to discern what had passed between them.

'What've you been saying to the boy?' he asked.

'Lighten up, Da. Samuel and me's mates. We've been having a wee talk, that's all.'

'Samuel wants nothing to do with your world, William, so don't try to poison him with your hate.'

Billy shook his head and started to move out of the room, then stopped and turned back to his father.

'The only poisonous thing in this house is all those crazy ideas you carry round in your head and you'll not be helping the boy or anyone else if you start to fill his head with them. What are those ledgers doing out? Do you think that's going to help the kid, showing him what's in those?'

They were arguing now and their rising voices speared his senses. The old man was holding onto one of the ledgers as if he expected someone might try to take it away. Their voices grew louder – vicious volleys of words – until he could stand it no more, and he slipped off the chair and ran through the kitchen to the back door, conscious only of the voice on the radio, and as he struggled with the handle he heard the voice break into laughter. Even as he ran into the garden and through the gap in the hedge, the mocking laughter ran alongside him and matched him step for step.

He could see his mother working in the kitchen and wondered why she did not look up at the sound of the laughter, but then as he focused on her, it raced finally round his head and swirled away like water down a drain. She smiled at him when he entered, but he could tell that she was agitated, and she prepared the evening meal with a staccato sharpness that told him something was wrong, clattering the lids of pots and letting cupboard doors bang as she closed them. He sat on one of the kitchen chairs and watched her. He seemed to notice more grey hairs each time he looked, and although he could not see her face it was obvious that she was upset. There was an open letter on the other side of the table, but it was folded so that it was not possible to read it. The more he wondered if this was the reason for her present mood, the more he grew curious about the contents, and after a while his hand edged towards it.

'Don't touch what doesn't concern you!' she snapped.

He drew back his hand guiltily and looked away as she lifted the letter and envelope, crumpled them bitterly in her hand, then crammed them into the pocket of her apron.

'There's some very sick people in the world. You'd have to be sick to go to the trouble of finding out where we'd moved to and writing filth like this. Isn't what they did to us enough without having to do this?'

He waited for her to tell him more but she turned again to the cooker and only the rigid line of her back betrayed her anger. He did not understand but he could tell that she was not going to say any more about it.

'Why don't you set the table instead of sitting there with your two arms the one length?'

Obediently he began to do as she had asked, lifting out the knives and forks so that nothing rattled and arranging them silently in the setting that always reminded them of the missing place. He could still see the crumpled letter and he found it difficult to take his eyes away from it. He opened the fridge, lifted out an unopened bottle of milk, the glass cold on his hands, and as he did so the bottle slipped through his fingers and shattered on the floor, jagged peaks of glass jutting out of the milky sea like tiny icebergs. Suddenly, his mother dropped what she was holding and grabbed him by the shoulders.

'Look what you've done – can you not be more careful?'

She was shaking him but it was the fierce frenzy of her face which shocked him more than anything, and he closed his eyes and tried to scream against it, but his voice froze in his throat and the only sounds were his mother's broken breathing, and the thumping of his heart. Then, as her hands slipped away, he darted past her and out through the door. She was calling to him, but as he ran her voice was replaced by the mocking laughter. Without slowing down, he squirmed through the gap in the fence at the bottom of the garden and clambered up the slope, the long seeded heads of grass wavering all about him, and he ran until a pain burned in his side and his breath came in great heaving gasps. He made his way, more slowly now, to the blunt-faced outcrop of rock and squeezed himself into a narrow fissure which ran deep into the stone, pushing his back tightly against the solid safety of the rock.

He felt more alone now than he had ever done before, alone and frightened of what the coming days would bring. There was no pattern now, no future road which he could travel with any expectation of arriving at some better place. The days ahead fused into a maze of misery where he and his mother wandered with increasing bitterness and despair. Soon they would begin to blame each other, their hurt rubbing against each other, keeping the memory raw and open. He could taste the misery but he could think of nothing to block out the weight of its inevitability, and then gradually his fear turned to anger, and he pushed his back against the cold surface of the rock and dug his heels into narrow ridges as if he was trying to throw the whole hill back over on itself. His brow furrowed with the strain and his teeth bit deep into his lower lip until a little tear of blood surfaced. He held the strain for as long as he could, then released it with an explosion of breath.

Nothing had moved, nothing had changed, and then in his anger he thought of the worst words in the world – the ugly, forbidden words he had never used and had seen written only on walls, and in his silent world he explored their unfamiliar taste, singly at first, waiting for some punishment, but when none came he grew bolder, chanting them over and over to himself until the pain was numbed. Then, lifting his face to the narrow strip of sky above him, he let them out in a wordless scream.

WORDS STREAMED OUT and through him like water, flooding and coursing through him, sweeping away all the barriers which separated him from the will of God, cleansing and irrigating the secret drought-ridden places of doubt. They washed over him, carrying him on a wave of release as words, strange words, bubbled to his lips in an overflowing of the inner spirit, and his head rocked from side to side, while his feet shuffled in a little dance of exultation. He lifted his open hands skywards and his feet moved steadily, rubbing the open threads of the oil-smeared carpet. Guttural noises formed in his throat and swam quiveringly into freedom as he spoke in tongues of mystery, his eyes rolling in his head and stipples of spit splashing his face.

The flecked light of the garage fanned about him, flowing round his convulsive movements and forming again as gradually his motion slowed and melted into a fragile stillness. His head lowered to his chest and his hands dropped lifelessly to his sides, only his feet lingering in a final spasm. He slumped onto the paint-smeared wooden

145

chair and his head flopped from side to side as if his neck was broken. Things were clearer now, with uncertainties swept away and his resolution washed clean and sure.

He looked about him, his eyes searching the dark corners and hidden places with a new-found courage. He would put off the moment no longer. He approached the secret place and began to lift away the coiled wreath of objects which concealed it. They felt strange to the touch, almost as if he was holding them for the first time and his hands shook a little as he set them down in the ritual pattern he had always followed. He had to force himself to open the back of the television set and then his hands searched with increasing desperation to find what he was looking for. His hands fluttered like the wings of a bird but he knew already that it was no longer there. For a second he tried to deceive himself with explanations, but the spirit of truth was upon him and he saw with clarity what it meant.

Standing back from the empty shell, he wiped the moisture from his lips with the back of his hand, and with unblinking eyes stared into the hollowed hiding place. Before, he had tried to deny it, to push it deeper into the shadows of his mind, but it had lingered there like an open sore. It had been a sin, nothing could be hidden from the light of the Spirit, and its rotting corpse could no longer be allowed to come close to the purity of what he must do. His task was too important and now its time had finally come, he could not risk it being tainted by the smear of evil.

Quickly, almost mechanically, he put everything back in its original position, conscious that he was doing it for the last time. He felt tired, very tired, almost as if he was coming to the final stages of a long journey. Suddenly, he spun round, his eyes darting everywhere, certain that someone was watching. But only the webbed crevices of silence stared back at him. He angled his head, listening for any sound that might have betrayed a presence, but he heard nothing except a far-off car. When he went out he did not bother to lock the door behind him but made his way into the house and climbed the stairs, his hand grasping the smooth surface of the wooden banister for support, and his breath coming in broken wheezes. If he had left it too late he knew that he would not be forgiven. He and the boy had been chosen to bring about the healing and yet if they were to do this holy thing their own lives had to be pure and free from any taint of sin. For too long he had sought to deny the truth about his son, hoping against hope that God's touch would save him, but he knew it was too late now – his son had turned his back on God's truth and could not be reached.

The door of his son's bedroom was closed and his hand hesitated before opening it. He had not slept at home for a couple of nights and opposite an unmade bed the curtains were still closed. He opened them just wide enough to let some light into the room, then turned suddenly, feeling once more that someone was watching him, but he stood alone in the small room, surrounded by the sprawl of his son's possessions. He began with the wardrobe, flicking through the assortment of coats and jackets, checking in all of their pockets, then pulling clothes out of the top shelf and dropping them in a pile on the floor. His hands clutched expectantly at a cardboard box buried under the last articles of clothing, but when his nervous fingers flicked open the lid, a confetti shower of tiny jigsaw pieces sprinkled to the floor. He flung the empty box into the wardrobe and went to the dresser, pulling out drawers with increasing desperation. Their contents piled up in layers about the floor but he was mindless of the growing confusion. At the back of the bottom drawer he found a locked wooden box – he hadn't seen it for maybe twenty years, but he recognized it as a box he had given his son as a child.

He tried to force the lid open with his hands but it was too solid, so he rummaged again through the dresser looking for a key. But there was none to be found and he tried again with his hands until his face tightened with the strain. It was no use. He looked around him and saw a screwdriver sitting on top of a partially dismantled amplifier and used it to lever open the lid. Wearied by his efforts, he sat down on the end of the bed and examined the contents. There were five or six blue-coloured envelopes fastened together by an elastic band. He opened the first one – it was a letter from some girl he had never heard of – read the first few lines and then set them on the bed. Underneath was a series of school reports but he did not open them, and below these a football medal with his son's name engraved on the back of it, and a few foreign coins. He was about to close the box when he found an old black and white photograph. It was his son as a baby in his mother's arms. It had been taken at Christmas and in the background could be seen the tiny silver tree they had used every year. He tried to remember taking the photograph but the years blurred into confusion. Perhaps it was their first Christmas with the boy, perhaps it was later. He could not remember.

He put it back in the box and shut the lid. It all belonged in the past and the past was something which no longer had any meaning. All that mattered now were the coming hours and days. He knew it was that close. But before that moment could begin, he had to put his own house in order and do the thing which he had avoided for too long. He let the box drop to the floor and continued his search, pulling posters off the walls and crumpling them into ragged balls in rising frustration. Records and books avalanched onto the spreading heap. He pulled the clothes off the bed and threw them into a corner, then lifted up the pillows and mattress. As he stood still and stared round the room, struggling a little to get his breath back, his eye caught the photograph which had spilled out of the box, the two faces in it watching him. He knelt down beside it, afraid to touch it, and then as he turned his face away he saw the raised edge of the carpet under the bed. It flapped back effortlessly under his touch like a page in a book, revealing the wooden floorboards underneath, and he could see without touching them that one was loose, but he rocked back on his knees, unwilling for a second to find out what was concealed.

It lifted out smoothly and completely, revealing only a pair of black woollen gloves. He sat back on the edge of the bed and looked at them, trying to remember if he had ever seen them before. Once, he had sheltered behind self-deception, but he knew now if he tried to hold fast to the lie it would be the harbinger of his own failure. Then, as he fidgeted with one of the gloves, he touched a tiny piece of rolled paper pushed up inside one of the fingers. It was rolled tightly like a cigarette paper and his hands found it difficult at first to find the opening edge. Unrolled, it was only a few inches square, and written on it in black ink was a list of four names. He read them slowly and carefully, but they held no meaning for him. He read them again, this time aloud, the heavy emphasis of his voice trying to force some significance from them, but they squatted on the page, indifferent to his efforts: John Connolly, Anthony McCallan, Sean Hughes, Francis Bradley.

Rising from the bed, he pulled the curtains fully open, making his eyes blink at the sudden light. As he stared down into the city, where each day more people were bitten by the serpents of fire, he heard the voice of the boy speaking to him, telling him what he must do, and the words filled him with fear.

He descended the stairs carefully, one hand clutching the banisters, the other, the tiny piece of paper. Half-way down, he paused as if reluctant to go any further, but then forced himself forward. In the living-room he opened the cupboard, took out the ledgers and laid them on the table. He opened the piece of paper and smoothed it flat: John Connolly, Anthony McCallan, Sean Hughes, Francis Bradley.

He found Hughes first. The date was only five weeks earlier, but the name had already passed from memory. There was no photograph of the man but he held his face close to the newspaper cutting, his lips moving deliberately as his finger probed the words like a blind man's stick: . . . SHOT IN FRONT OF HIS FAMILY AS THEY WERE HAVING

SUPPER. TWO MASKED MEN ENTERED THROUGH THE UNLOCKED KITCHEN DOOR AND SHOT HIM REPEATEDLY . . . DIED INSTANTLY . . . FOUR-YEAR-OLD DAUGHTER WAS GRAZED BY A BULLET . . . THE FAMILY HAVE CALLED FOR NO REVENGE.

It took him a few minutes to find McCallan, a taxi driver who had picked up two fares and driven them to some waste-ground where they shot him in the back of the head as he sat in his driver's seat. A single man who lived with his mother. There was a photograph of a winding cortège of taxis.

He turned back more pages and found John Connolly. His badly beaten body had been found in an alley behind a leisure centre. LAST SEEN DRINKING IN A SOCIAL CLUB IN THE NEW LODGE AREA. HIS FAMILY DENY THAT HE HAD ANY CONNECTION WITH PARAMILITARIES. There was a photograph of Connolly, a man in his early fifties with a spray in his lapel. Taken at a wedding probably, maybe his son's or daughter's.

As he read the cuttings he felt a fist of sickness clench in his stomach. So much shedding of blood and now some of it was splashed on his hands, the very hands that were supposed to bring healing. He stumbled into the kitchen and hunched over the sink, then spattered his face with water and without drying it, turned back to the table. There was one more name he had to find.

At first he turned the pages slowly, scrutinizing each cutting, but soon his fingers flicked through them feverishly as he searched more frantically. Further back in time, through the years, one ledger after another and then forward again to the present, but no Francis Bradley. It had to be there, recorded along with the three others, because he had carried out his task faithfully and unerringly. Droplets of water dripped onto the pages, doubling their size as they soaked into the newsprint. Francis Bradley. He repeated it again and again, trying to summon it from the host of names, but it could not be found, and then he understood the reason. Francis Bradley was still alive. Somewhere down in the ravelled rows of streets, Francis Bradley was living his life, unaware that his name was on a tiny piece of paper hidden below floorboards. Then he heard the beating of the dark angel's wings as it moved from door to door. Perhaps it was already too late. He crumpled the piece of paper once more and placed it carefully in the fire, watching as the flames consumed it.

Was it too late? He remembered his son's radio in the kitchen and he lurched away from the table, knocking over the chair as he went. When he switched the radio on, discordant music screamed at him, mocking his frustrated fumbling with the dial as he searched for a speaking voice, but his fingers only pushed it in and out of static. Spitting, hissing voices and broken snatches of song broke from the wavebands of the night. It was no use. He switched it off, and then, in the brittle silence, he heard once more the boy's whispering voice. It was calling him, telling him to stay close, telling him that the time had finally come.

Hurriedly, he put on his overcoat and got ready, pausing only to take a black-handled knife from the kitchen drawer and drop it noiselessly into his pocket.

'I'VE BEEN THINKING about it for some time now, Samuel. I think we should go back home.'

His mother paused and looked at him, trying to gauge his reaction and when he looked into her face he knew that she was serious about what she said.

'I've given it a lot of thought and a lot of prayer, and I feel it would be best for us to go back and live where we used to. Not in the same house, because we couldn't, of course, but somewhere in that area. Somewhere in the country, close to the church and the people we know.'

He knew the admission of failure was painful for her and that it had taken a long time to bring her to this moment. He glanced away from her face and out to the ice where the crowds of skaters circled the rink in a constant procession.

'It just hasn't worked here. I don't know why, or if it's my fault, but things just haven't worked. I thought at the start it would be better for us − better for you − but something's gone wrong with it. I thought it would be a fresh start, a chance to pick up the pieces and begin again.'

She paused once more and he knew she was talking to the silent parts of herself as well as to him.

'If anything, I think it made things worse. It's not the place I remember. Everything's changed and you can't build a new life on memories. I know my family visits us, but it's not like we really know anybody and I just don't think I want to live here.'

Out on the ice, the skilled skaters gathered speed and wove in and out of the slower groups.

'It hasn't helped you, Samuel, has it? You still have the dreams, you still feel the fear. Running away didn't change anything for either of us, didn't help us forget, or make the pain any less. It was a mistake, but I thought I was doing it for the best and I was too ready to listen to other people. They meant well enough, but at the end of the day all it amounted to was running away.'

She was trying not to cry and he took her hand and held it tightly. She bit her bottom lip and nodded her head slowly as if to say that shedding any more tears was pointless and she was not going to be weak.

'And why should we run away? It's not us that have anything to be ashamed of, it's not us that need to hide our faces from the world. It's our home and why should we let those types of people drive us out of it? At the end of the day, that's just what they want – for all of us to be scared and leave the towns and farms for those who never did anything to build them. Why should we let them think they've won? I think, Samuel, we should sell the house and go back, hold our heads high and be brave for your father's sake.'

She was watching him for some sign but he felt confused. He didn't want to go back, but he didn't want to stay. Instead, he wanted to live in some different place, but he didn't know where that place was. He wanted to find some secret door and pass through it into some safer, better world where there were no men with nothing in their eyes.

'There's something else wrong with this place. It's hard to describe it because it's something you can't touch or see, but it's there all the time, a feeling that it's sitting on the edge of something more terrible than anything that's gone before.'

She flicked hair that was not there away from her eyes.

'Maybe that sounds stupid – I don't know. I don't know very much for sure any more.'

Her free hand plucked at invisible specks of fluff on her skirt. He felt she was talking to him as she had never done before, but he knew he could not be brave for her or his father because there was no protection in bravery. Better to grow small and safe, hide where cruel hands could not reach. His mother still believed that God would look after them, but he knew that God did not care and would do nothing to help them.

Out on the ice the skating circle went round and round. She motioned him out onto the ice and although he was reluctant to leave her she urged him to join the skaters. She seemed to want to be on her own for a while, so carefully holding the rail with both hands, he took little sideways steps and manoeuvred himself onto the ice.

She had brought him here as a treat and as a way of saying sorry for what had happened, but he had never blamed her. It had been the fault of the letter, the crumpled letter with its spider writing.

He took small cautious steps at first, his legs stiff and still unaccustomed to balancing on the narrow blades, but it was easier than he had imagined and so far he had only fallen once, two tiny spots of damp bearing witness to his brief moment on the ice. His arms jutted from his sides as if he was walking a tightrope and his face was taut with concentration as he stayed close to the side, his eyes fixed mostly on the ice, lifting occasionally to check that the way ahead was clear. Gradually, as his confidence increased, some of the rigidity vanished from his legs and he began to push each foot out with greater fluency, and his hesitant movements took on the characteristics of a glide. He began to push more of himself into the forward motion, straightening and relaxing as it carried him across the ice, and as he completed a circuit and drew level with his mother, she waved to him and encouraged him to keep going.

He set off again, feeling bold enough to increase his speed. All around him were other young people, many of them dressed in fluorescent colours, some of them experienced skaters, but also many no more competent than himself. Sometimes people stumbled or fell across his path and he had to glide round them. He had almost got the hang of turning and was beginning to understand how to use his body when he wanted to veer from a straight line. As he poured himself into his forward motion he thought of the home they had left and the places where he had grown up, and for some reason he did not understand, he thought of the swallows – dark spurts of speed stitching the sky, the swallows that came back every summer and relined their nests under the eaves. They would have gone by now, leaving behind their secret nests for another year. He thought, too, of the hedgerows and the lanes where he had strolled, stick in hand, beheading tall weeds; of the dam built in the stream – a barrier of mud and stone, and the suds of scum on the top of the water, white, like hawthorn.

He glided on, pushing himself deeper into the rhythm. His mother was right – they did not belong in Belfast. Perhaps what the old man had said about the sickness was true. Maybe there was a sickness spreading to more people every day, spreading until it covered everywhere, just like the spider writing covered every surface, and maybe if they stayed here much longer they too would be infected. He remembered the night he had seen the fires, and as he followed the cold scratches of the ice, he imagined a great fire being built and lit in the darkness, so big that no one could put it out or stop it consuming everything which crossed its path.

It would not be easy going back, and he remembered the frieze of faces which had lurked in the walls of his room and the whispering voices which wound their tightening grip round the trembling silences of the house. It would not be easy, but he thought, too, of his father's grave in the church cemetery and it seemed solitary and lonely. The flowers would be withered now, blown everywhere by the wind; it felt as though they had somehow deserted him, had been only thinking of themselves. He knew, too, that if they stayed in the city something bad would happen to their lives. He did not know how it would end, but each day that went by loosened his mother's hold on things and she grew, not stronger, but more fragile. Maybe it was the sickness. With a sudden quiver of fear he wondered if it had already infected them. He looked up and all about him he could hear the music and laughter spurring on the whirl of skaters. There were so many people and all of them strangers in his life. Some of them skated arm-in-arm, others formed chains, but no one linked with him or touched him as they passed. He looked over to where his mother was sitting and for a second felt a tight press of panic when he could not see her. As he searched the rows of seats his concentration faltered and he almost slipped, but regained his balance just as he spotted her. She had moved away for a few moments to buy some drinks. She beckoned him over with her hand and he put his arms out in front of him to act as brakes. When he sat down his legs felt funny, the same way they did when he dismounted from a bicycle after cycling hard. She handed him the drink and he cupped it in his hands and sipped it slowly.

'I know the day we set out for Belfast I told you it was for the best, so I suppose you don't have much confidence in my judgement any more, but the more I think about it, the more I feel it was wrong for us. Your uncle says they're building nice new bungalows just outside the village, and they're not so big that we'd rattle around inside them like two peas in a pod.'

Out on the ice a girl did an elaborate spin, ravelling and unravelling herself with effortless ease.

158

'I wish you were able to tell me what you think, Samuel. I want to do what's best for you and I know you'll tell me everything in your own time, but it's hard deciding these things by myself. I suppose I'm used to making important decisions with your father, so it feels strange now to have to do it on my own. But a lot of things feel strange now. Maybe if we went home it would be a help to you, Samuel. Maybe things would get better for you more quickly.'

He took her hand and led her towards the ice. She was reluctant at first, claiming that she was no good at it, but when he insisted she went with him. They set off slowly, hand in hand, his mother taking small diffident steps, almost as if she was attempting to walk across the ice, and he could feel the tightness of her grip as she held onto him for support. Once, she wobbled and he thought for a second that she was going to fall, but they clutched each other and found a faltering balance before setting off again. She began to smile and relax a little as they circled the rink.

'This reminds me of the day your aunt and I won the three-legged race at Portrush. Only I think we must've been moving a bit faster than this.'

A man and his young daughter – she couldn't have been more than five or six years old – skated past and smiled at them.

'Some people make it look so easy they'd put you to shame, and yet to look at me now you wouldn't think that I'd done this before. We went skating a couple of times up in the King's Hall in the old days. It was all the go for a while.'

When they completed a circuit she felt she had done enough and made her way to the seats, but she insisted that he should keep going for another while. He watched her as she went to return her skates and when she was out of sight he set off again. Somewhere deep inside himself he felt a tiny tremor of happiness as he locked himself into the rhythm once more, and deliberately he gave himself up to it, pushing with the pulse of his being, letting his spirits glide. It tasted cold and sweet as his blades carved a fine tracery of crystal and all about him the ice sparkled with diamond scratches. Everyone faded out of his consciousness and he felt like a tiny stone skimming the white-crested waves, never pausing long enough to sink below the water. Pushing and gliding, propelling himself forward in a perfect rhythm, never stumbling or losing his balance, using his arms to drive himself on. He made himself think of the good things that had happened in his life, polishing them in his memory like a stone found on the beach. Scoring them into the ice, a tumble of bright images garlanding his head like blossom – the tractor lights shooting moth-filled spears of light into the darkness; the house decorated with Christmas holly his mother had cut from the back hedge; sledging in the big field in winter snow. Maybe it could be like this, maybe he did not have to find another world to live in if he could spark his own momentum which would carry him forward, skimming over the shimmering surface of his life, never pausing long enough for the clutching hands to fasten onto him. Just maybe, he could score his own good memories deep enough to block the sound of his screams, silence the whispering voices.

He felt a tiny bud of hope open in his heart – he could go wherever his mother wanted, support her in the days ahead. He started to skate faster still, but just at that moment he was aware of something happening on the far side of the rink. People were suddenly falling and tripping over each other, some laughing, others shouting angrily, and, as if in his worst dreams, a dark figure, arms flapping like the wings of a black crow, was stumbling towards him. It called him by name as it fell to the ice, scrambled upright again and lurched towards him once more.

HIS FEET SLITHERED from beneath him and the ice burnt the palms of his hands as he tried to push himself up again. He scrambled up as more people tripped over the sprawling bodies which littered his wake. White frosted crystals starred his black coat and damp circles darkened on his knees as he stumbled on shakily. People were shouting at him but he raised his voice above the clamour and called to the boy, stretching out his arms in invitation, calling his name as laughter and anger surged all around him. Across the ice the boy's pale moon face was frozen into stillness, his red hair a burning halo of holiness. And then, as his feet slipped once more from below him, he felt hands grabbing him and pulling him to his feet, forcing him away from the boy and off the ice. The harder he struggled, the firmer the hands gripped him, and when he sagged they pulled him back to his feet and bundled him forward.

They carried him into an office and pushed him into a seat. Some of them were smiling at him while others standing behind his back joked to each other. They were young men about the same age as his own son and in their faces he saw that they too were blinded by their sin. He knew he could not make them understand, knew that none of his words would reach them, that their only hope now was to look in faith at the serpent of brass which God was going to raise up.

A man in a suit arrived and asked him questions but he answered none of them and when the young men laughed to each other and called him 'Grandpa' he still said nothing. The man in the suit talked about calling the police but eventually said he would let him off with a warning. As he looked around at the mocking faces he felt no bitterness, only a well of sympathy for these young men whose hearts had been hardened and who marched blindly onwards, oblivious to their coming fate. One of them patted him on the back and brushed his coat a little, then two of them took him by his arms and led him to an exit, opening the door and guiding him down the steps before releasing him. As he looked up at the neon signs on the front of the building they dazzled his eyes.

'Next time you want to go on the ice, Grandpa, hire a pair of skates.'

He stood listening as their laughter disappeared inside the building. Around him the night shook with an immediacy which disturbed him – the high wail of voices, the lights of arriving cars, crowds of rushing people. He pushed past them, searching for some silent, shadowy respite and as he set off into the falling darkness, his hand fingered the blade of the knife nestling in his pocket and his fingers explored its sharp coldness. It felt beautiful to his touch, colder than the ice, sharper than any human truth.

Into his memory flickered an image of his wife's cavernous face, her sunken eyes deep pools of suffering and the brittle coils of grey wreathed on the pillow, and he saw clearly what he had to do. He thought of Sean Hughes, of John Connolly, a man with a white spray in his lapel, of Anthony McCallan and the winding cavalcade of taxis. He thought of Francis Bradley, perhaps at that very moment living his life, talking to his wife, touching his children, unaware that his name had been called, added to a list by people he would never know, people he would see only once. All across the city that summer the beating of the dark angel's wings, moving through the narrow streets and white-walled estates, stopping at doors which had been singled out by men with no faces. Lintels smeared with blood.

As the falling dusk thickened about him he walked steadily until he reached a main road and caught a bus towards the city centre, and then another which took him home. As he climbed the roads up to his house he had to stop at regular intervals to regain his breath. He felt more weary now than he had ever done in his whole life. Above him the night sky was a dark net stretched taut, shivering stars trapped in the mesh. The house was silent; the curtains of his son's room were still open and the grey square of glass stared blindly down at him. As he opened the gate he caught the scent of stock and white alyssum glistened like patches of frost. He walked down the side of the house, pushed open the unlocked door, and stood listening, his head raised and alert. A droplet of water dripped into the sink and somewhere pipes stretched a little, but the house hunched over him, an empty husk of a home. It frightened him a little and he felt only hostility in the things that should have been familiar and reassuring. He avoided touching anything, pulling his coat tightly about him so that he did not brush anything as he passed.

In the living-room the fire was out, and the ledgers still squatted on the table. He could not bring himself to put on the lights, but stood motionless until his eyes grew accustomed to the greyness. He forced himself to climb the stairs, each step a battle against his will, taking him closer to a confirmation of something which even at this final hour he hoped might still be taken from him. On the landing grey swirls of light ebbed and flowed about him and the open door of his son's room signalled him forward.

It had not been a dream. All around him were still strewn the clothes and possessions he had scattered a few hours earlier. They lay in heaped piles at his feet while opened drawers sagged into the space below them. His eyes picked out the blue envelopes lying beside the wooden box and then he saw the photograph. He sat down on the edge of the bed and held it close to his face. He could remember it now. The camera had been borrowed from someone at work. It had been that first Christmas. The boy was only six months old and round the tiny silver tree were the presents she had wrapped for him. He had teased her about the care with which she had wrapped them when she knew the child was too young to open them and she would have to undo all her own careful work. So much happiness, so many hopes and dreams all bound together in the little photograph. Where had it all gone? He stared into the faces. Was there always some tare in the wheat, some seed of corruption present even in that very moment? Had it always been there, growing steadily and stealthily, unperceived because he did not want to see it or acknowledge its existence? He slipped the photograph into the pocket of his coat and went down the stairs.

Outside, the night air had grown colder and the sky looked like a net that might fall at any moment. On his way to the garage he glanced up at the boy's house but there were no lights on. The unlocked door of the garage opened noiselessly and he stared into the darkness for a second before he went in, carefully closing the door behind him. As he approached the secret place he knew already that nothing had been touched. He looked around at the things which had once played some part in his life but were now decaying in damp corners, forgotten about. He moved around, his feet shuffling noiselessly across the carpet, touching things with a vague curiosity as if trying to recapture some lost meaning. Then, finding the best place he began to move objects, making a little path into the corner of the garage's back wall. He lifted the wooden chair and sat down on it in the cleared space, his head resting against an old bookcase which was now used to store tins of nails and screws. Then gradually the disturbance which his movements had created died away, and the stillness engulfed him and blended him with the webbed world of silence. He could smell the rotting grass which clogged the roller of the mower and lined the crevices of the grassbox, and then slowly his eyes closed and he slipped into a shallow sleep.

He journeyed into the past to a day when it felt

as if the whole scent of summer was in the flowers. Surprised to see them, surprised and proud . . . drinking the lemonade she had brought . . . showing the child off to the other workmen. He could taste the sweetness of the day, hear the child's laughter as the swing carried them higher, just a little higher each time, his arms outstretched to catch them both. Into the past on a warm slipstream of memory.

Suddenly, he started, his head jerking upright, his eyes staring wildly into the shadows. Someone outside was trying to unlock the already-open door. His lips moved in a frenzy of prayer, hoping even now that God would take away this bitter cup. He stood up and pushed his back against the wall. Some other way, some lamb in the thicket. He stood, imperceptible and motionless, while the door opened and a vague, ill-defined figure entered, its sudden, hurried movements scattering the stillness. He pushed his back more tightly against the wall, the plaster cold as the ice on the palms of his hands. It felt as though they were burning as he gripped the wall for support.

He watched as the figure began to uncover the secret place and in the greyness he saw a bright flash of the oilskinned package and he knew then what he had always known. He stepped forward out of his hiding place, the voices in his head growing louder and more insistent with each step he took until they pounded like hammers in his head. The oil-stained carpet softened his tread as he moved to within a few feet of the stooping figure and suddenly, without warning, the shadowy shape spun round and there was a gleam of a pale face in the gloom. The package clattered to the floor.

'What the hell –'

He was close enough to see the look of recognition in his son's eyes replace the first jolt of fear.

'In the name of God, Da, what're you doing standing there like some ghost? What the hell do you think you're doing?'

No other way, no lamb in the thicket. Stretching out his arm he rested it gently on his son's shoulder, then pulled him close.

'I loved you, William,' he whispered.

There was no scream, just a sudden spasm and a gurgling noise as the body slumped forward into his arms. He held on to it tightly until the final jerk had ended. Blood was still coming from his son's mouth as he laid him down on the threadbare carpet, then knelt over him, rocking back and forward as he lightly cradled his head.

'I loved you,' he whispered. 'It would have been just like it was before. You remember what it was like – the cancer eating away her body day by day, her eyes brimming with pain. I can't let this sickness spread any more, can't let it infect more and more people.'

He sat holding his son for a long time, rocking in the dust-filled darkness, and then he heard the voices speaking to him once more, but their words twisted and turned and were like the radio's confused crackling of static. He stroked his son's hair as if he was a sleeping child, then slowly stood up. The package lay where it had fallen. He pushed it into his pocket and went out, locking the door behind him.

As he turned away he glanced up at the boy's house.

There were lights on now, and somewhere the boy was there. The whispering spoke to him about the boy but he could not be sure what they wanted him to do. Perhaps now the boy himself was contaminated, his purity tainted and besmirched by the sickness. The voices in his head were like tongues of fire and he put both hands to his temples in an attempt to soothe the pain. He felt the warm blood on his hands and dropped them to his side, wiping them on the front of his coat, and then with a final look at the lights in the boy's house, he staggered into the night, his mouth moving constantly as it framed silent prayers.

Time now ceased to exist and without knowing how he got there, he found himself walking the embankment, following the black snake of the river, its skin glazed with neon. The water seemed to have no motion or movement except the silvery tremble of its surface as he stopped on the bridge and stared down at it. So much darkness in the heart of man, so much sickness. The voices had faded now and he knew that he had failed God, had not been worthy of His calling. The knowledge chilled him with a shiver of shame and his hands gripped the parapet for support. A trembling sheen of white light fastened on the water below. From his pocket he took the oilskinned package and dropped it into the secret depths, only a brief splash of white marking its entry into the water. His hand touched something else – the photograph. He clutched it as though it was something sacred, something he could carry with him on his journey.

THE OLD MAN's house was still and silent. It was already mid-morning and yet there was no sign of him. The boy wondered if something had happened because of what he had done at the ice rink the night before. He did not understand what the old man had wanted, but he knew he would never harm anyone and he felt, too, that if the old man had got into trouble it was because of him. As he looked around the garden they had worked on and almost rescued from neglect, he wondered where the men had taken him. A strong wind was blowing and it pulled at the heads of the flowers they had planted. Only the red spears of salvia stood steady against it. An empty plastic pot rolled across the lawn until it was trapped by the roots of the hedge, and a polythene bag which was also caught, inflated like a balloon. Across the bottom of the garden the blackened trees bent over at crazy angles. Perhaps the old man had decided not to work in the garden, perhaps he was resting somewhere in his house.

He looked up at it with curiosity. Outwardly it looked

no different from all the other houses, maybe a little shabbier, but that was all. A few blistered flakes of plaster moved in the wind and a wire which came from an upstairs window and ended without purpose, flapped loose, snapping like a whip. He stood in the gap in the hedge, his head level with its top, and pulled at the branches, shredding leaves between his fingers and letting the wind carry them out of sight. Some of them stuck to his jumper and he brushed them off quickly as if they were dangerous insects.

There was no smoke coming from the chimney. As he looked at the house he began to think that he himself might be the cause of all the bad things that had happened in his life. His father had never done harm to anyone – he had heard his mother say it – so perhaps it was not his father whom God was punishing but himself. Maybe now the old man would also be punished because of him; maybe it was something about him that caused all these things to happen. But why should God single him out? What had he done to make God hate him so? He wondered if it was something terrible which God could see in his heart. And as the wind whipped past him, he remembered guiltily the words he had used in the cleft of the rock. Perhaps he could begin to love God, or even deceive Him with a pretence of love. But if God could really see everything and knew everything in the world He had created, then He would not be deceived. He tried to pray for forgiveness, to submit himself to God's will, but his thoughts flew up in all directions like birds scattered from a field. The old man often spoke of God, perhaps he might know how he could be forgiven and passed over in the days to come, how he might be erased from God's memory. But the old man was nowhere to be seen.

He moved out of the gap in the hedge and walked towards the house, the windows watching each step he took. The small kitchen window was slightly open and the curtains shivered in the draught. He knocked and peered through the frosted glass, putting his face so close that his nose pressed against its coldness, but no one came to answer. Inside he could see only a misted world receding into milky space. His hand gripped the door handle and without meaning to, he leaned his weight on it, pushing it open. It opened only a few inches. He did not go in, but stood looking into the exposed section of kitchen, where uncleared plates and cups sat on the table, and a filament of cracks ran down the wall. He knocked the open door again and the noise drummed in the silence before he pushed it fully open and stepped into the kitchen. A chair was lying on its back on the floor, but there was no sign of the old man.

He wondered if he should look in the living-room, but before he went any further into the house he turned to make sure that the door behind him was still open. He stepped slowly and quietly, moving stealthily through the silence that grew louder with each step he took. Everything in the room looked the way he remembered it except for the size. It seemed to have grown smaller, almost as if he could reach out his arms and touch the faded wallpaper, the worn furniture, the wedding photograph on the wall with the bride's face that could hardly be seen. The fire was a blackened smattering of cinders and ash and the whole house felt cold and damp. Outside he heard the wind rattling the lid of a dustbin and as he glanced back towards the kitchen once more, he saw that the open door was being blown slowly shut.

As his eyes fastened on the green ledgers on the table he felt an urge to leave. Somewhere above him the wind disturbed rafters and slates and suddenly he grabbed the top ledger and ran out the way he had come, almost tripping over the fallen chair in his haste to be gone. Pulling the back door shut behind him, he pressed his face once more to the opaque glass, staring to see if any dark shape was striding after him, but after a few seconds he turned away and walked back down the garden.

He paused at the garage, wondering if perhaps the old man might be working inside, but when he tried the door he found that it was locked, and he pushed at it roughly with his hands. He wondered why the old man took so much care to keep it locked when it looked as if it contained nothing of value. He fiddled with the bolt but knew he would not be able to open it, and then noticing a thin rip in one of the curtains, he put the ledger down on the path and, placing his forearms on the window, scrambled his feet against the brick, until his head was level with the tiny hole. He squinted into the gloom but all he could distinguish was the vague outline of things stacked against the far wall. Only able to support his weight for a few seconds, he dropped back onto the ground, and as he picked up the ledger, he noticed that he had scuffed the toes of both his shoes. He bent over and spat on them, then rubbed them with the pulled-down cuff of his jumper.

If anything, the wind had grown stronger and so he clutched the ledger tightly as he climbed over the back wall into the fields in case it should be snatched from his hands. The ragged grass quivered all around him as the wind quickened it and set it spinning in wavering patterns, and his free hand snapped shut on streaming thistledown before releasing them on their journey once more. The wind was behind, billowing his clothes and pushing him on. Half-way there he stopped for a rest and looked back to where smoke spiralled angrily from chimneys. The grass was damp and fine wisps of water latticed his trousers. As he set off again his pace slowed as he reached the steepest part of the slope, and he used his free hand to push his knee into the incline, working it like a piece of machinery. When he reached the outcrop he touched the cold surface of the stone and traced the raised ridges of its surface with the tips of his fingers. Tiny tufts of velvety moss lined the cracks and it seemed to him that the rock was something very old. Wriggling his way into the fissure he pushed his back tightly into the crevice, and in the narrow gap above his head he could see the open sky and windswept clouds racing across it.

He pulled his knees up towards his chest and propped the ledger against them. He was not sure why he had taken it and now as he looked at its cover, it reminded him of the books the police had shown him. Books with faces in them – the faces he carried round in his head and which he could not forget, no matter how hard he tried. But none of them had been the men who had killed his father. He found it hard to remember clearly what they looked like. Only the eyes of the man who had looked at him remained clear in his memory – empty, pupilless eyes, like grey seas where no fish swam; on a summer's evening, cold as the rock that his hand now touched. He wondered where the man was now. Did he have a family? Maybe a wife, children of his own? How could they live with him, look into those eyes every day and not know what he had done? Probably he had killed before, and maybe he had killed again since that evening. He wondered, too, if the man ever thought of him, remembered what he looked like. He could never feel safe until he knew that both of them were dead, but how would he ever know that, when he did not know their names, or even remember their faces? Some day they might come back to seek him out, to kill him too. He knew they would come silently and quickly like that summer's evening when they had burst from the shelter of the hedgerow and moved through the soft-edged light of the setting sun. For the rest of his life he would have to hide, have to search strangers' faces to see if they were the ones.

He looked up at the sliver of sky. Summer was slipping away day by day. Once it had been the hub around which his whole year turned, with endless weeks of freedom stretching lazily into a boundless haze of pleasure, but now he was glad it was passing, and he looked forward to the days when advancing shadows would cover the world and hide it from the spying eyes of light. Soon, too, he would be going home. His mother had decided it was the best thing to do, but he no longer believed that any 'best thing' existed. No matter how hard he had looked, he had been unable to find the door which led into some different world. He could often see it in his imagination, just like some picture in a children's story, old and ivy-covered, disguised by age and ancient vines, set in a brick wall which was weathered and pock-marked, and when the rusted handle was turned it opened to reveal a secret world where nothing bad was ever able to enter. Perhaps there was no door because no such world existed, and never could, but why then did he go on looking for it, believing that he might be able to find it?

He fingered the cover of the ledger. The old man had said that God told him to record the names of the dead in it. As he moved his hand across it, he noticed a little yellow blister on his palm, a witness to how much spade-work he had done in recent weeks, and he pulled the raised skin off with his teeth, revealing a tiny weal of pink. It stung as he opened at the first page and started to read. A man ambushed as he drove down the lane to his farmyard. The newsprint had started to yellow and one of the edges was crinkled where it had not been smoothed out properly. They had lain in wait behind an old stone wall and shot him as he turned off the engine. He turned the page. A policeman shot in the back of his head as he visited his elderly mother. Another page. Three men shot dead in a dock-side bar after being singled out and everyone made to lie on the floor, blood and drink swilling round their bodies. A body found on waste-ground, the face battered with a breeze block beyond recognition. Another page. A man shot on a building site while he drank from a mug of tea; a seventeen-year-old girl killed as she left an evening service, her Bible in her hand; a man blown up in his car as he set out for work.

He read each story carefully, leaving nothing out and holding the ledger reverently as if it was a holy object. More pages. A taxi-driver shot as he waited to collect a mother and baby from hospital; a man dragged from a shopping centre in front of his wife and child and shot as he knelt in the carpark. Page after page of yellowing newsprint. Pictures of tarpaulin-covered bodies dumped in ditches under hedgerows; the twisted wreckage of burnt-out cars; tattered wreaths hanging from wire fences on country roads; cortèges with slow processions of people. Stories of ambush and bullet, of atrocity and revenge. Pictures, too, of the victims. He looked into their faces and tried to know them, but they had faded like their stories into the past. Sometimes there were small portraits, like passport photographs, but often their images were taken from family snapshots, preserved mementoes of weddings or celebrations which sat strangely beside the stories which surrounded them.

He paused from reading, using his thumb as a bookmark as he closed the ledger, while above him the wedge of sky darkened and dropped lower towards him. He pushed his back against the steadying support of stone, conscious that his breathing had quickened and a whirl of sickness was spinning wildly in his stomach. He tried to calm himself by counting, counting anything he could see – the eyelets on his shoes, the scores on the leather, bits of damp grass stuck to the soles – but all the time he knew he had to go on reading and with every page he turned, the newspaper cuttings carried him closer to the present. His reading had become slower and his mouth was dry but he moved through the years, and as he did so the paper began to lose its faded look. He started to close his eyes for the second it took his forefinger to flick over the next page and then the second lengthened and he had to make himself look.

It seemed to go on for a long time, a frightened game of roulette between hand and eye.

And then he reached it. He pushed as hard as he could against the rock, his heels dug into the ground and legs tightening with the strain. The sickness swirled in his stomach but he forced himself to look at the photograph. He had never seen it before, never known it existed. As he stared at his mother's face he recognized the marks of pain which now lived permanently in her features, and then as he looked at himself he saw the fear in his eyes, and in that moment everything came flooding back, breaching all his strongest barriers – birds scattering to the sky, the setting sun sinking into the dark ridge of the horizon, kneeling beside his father's head afraid to touch him, while his blood seeped into the stubble.

Suddenly, his hands tore at the pages of the ledger, plucking them from the spine and ripping them into shreds, pulling page after page and tearing them into pieces. The fragments fluttered around him like snow and, scooping them up, he pushed them through the gap above his head and watched the wind sweep them skywards. He looked about, frantic that the last fragment had gone, and then he saw that his hands were blackened with the print of the newspaper. He rubbed them violently on his trousers, but all it did was smear the print across his skin. He wanted the marks off his hands more than anything else, but the harder he rubbed the deeper it became engrained. He was crying now, slowly at first, and then in shuddering sobs which he could not control or stop, crying until there was nothing left except a heaving emptiness and the smell of his urine. The print would not come off his hands.

He had sat with his back pressed so hard against the rock that now it felt part of his spine and as he thought of the pages he had torn, he knew for sure that the old man was right. Down below in the scooped-out hollow of a city lived a terrible sickness and each day it spread to more people as the serpents slithered silently among them, infecting them with the poison. The old man had spoken of a cure but maybe it had existed only inside his head, buried amidst the tangle of words. Maybe Billy was right and words were only the shit of the world, empty meaningless things like dead leaves trapped in the spring grass.

The emptiness inside him felt so big it seemed that nothing could fill it, that nothing could ever deaden the pain. He watched a solitary bird fall through the sky. And then from somewhere deep inside his hurt he knew what he had to do without understanding why he had been chosen or what would happen to him. At first he tried to push the knowledge below the surface of his silence and he fought against it, wanting to go on hiding in the fissure of the rock, to grow small and safe like the stone in the ditch.

He crawled out of the crevice, his legs stiff and awkward at first, then clambered over the stone to the top of the outcrop. All about him the wind whipped through the grass. At first, he crouched low under the torn rag of a sky, but then he stood up slowly and nervously, like a hunted creature emerging from shadows, and looked down into the city; over the serried ridges of roofs, over the tall towers of the centre and across to the scattered scabs of estates blistering the far side of the hollow. As the wind broke coldly on his face and tore at his tousle of hair, he stretched out his arms and hovered weightlessly like a small bird. Unclenching his fists, he let the air beat against his print-blackened palms and rush through his open fingers.

He felt raised up above the world, high enough for all to see him, but down below it seemed the city still slumbered in its sickness, unwilling to lift its eyes. He grew desperate as the wind stabbed his clothes and sought to dislodge him from the stone. There was so little time left. Soon it might be too late, and in his desperation he reached deep into his sealed and secret places, slipping open the hoops of silence which bound him fast. And as he lifted his face words faltered in the fiery flux of his throat, each sound a tiny flame which seared the softness of his being. They stuttered brokenly to his lips, melting at first into nothingness like snow falling on water, but he forced them forward until at last they broke free. His voice rang out raw and strange, but he shouted again and again, calling the world to look, and as he hung trembling on the air, the wind scattered the words like seed.